Anonymous

Crispus

Anonymous

Crispus

ISBN/EAN: 9783337380663

Printed in Europe, USA, Canada, Australia, Japan

Cover: Foto ©Andreas Hilbeck / pixelio.de

More available books at **www.hansebooks.com**

CRISPUS,

THE

SON OF CONSTANTINE.

A TRAGEDY,

IN

FIVE ACTS.

By A. D.

NEW YORK.
1873.

CRISPUS.

PERSONS REPRESENTED.

Males:

CONSTANTINE, Roman Emperor.

CRISPUS, son to the Emperor, with the title of Cæsar.

SEMPRONIUS, the Emperor's confidant.

BASILIUS, a Patrician, in the favour of the Emperor.

MANNIUS,
PISANNIUS, } Patricians, and friends of Crispus.
LUCULLUS,

LACTANTIUS, an ecclesiastic, formerly tutor to Crispus.

BENEVOLENTIUS, a soldier, favoured by Crispus.

PAPPUS, an old man about the Palace.

An OFFICER of the GUARD.

CONSTANTIUS,
CONSTANS, } Half-brothers to Crispus.
CONSTANTINE the Younger,

      Courtiers, Soldiers, Attendants, &c.

Females:

FAUSTA, Empress, and stepmother to Crispus.

HELENA, daughter of Licinius, niece to Constantine.

OLD HELENA, the Emperor's mother.

SERVIA, maid to Helena.

      Ladies, Maids in Waiting, Servants, &c.

CRISPUS.

ACT I.

SCENE 1.—The Palace of Constantine, at Nicomedia.

Enter SEMPRONIUS *and* FAUSTA.

SEMP. I've spoken with the herald, who declares
That wheresoe'er he goes he is received
With shouts of "Long live Crispus!" "Long live Cæsar!"
Not e'en the Emperor's self, in youth or age,
Was ever welcomed with more rapturous joy.
The Cæsar, ere the sun sets, will be here.

FAUSTA. He never shall go back again to Gaul.
He is a cloud betwixt me and the sun,
Casting a shadow on myself and mine,
Himself absorbing all the golden light
That should have shed a lustre o'er my sons.
I've lived in vain to gain an emperor's love,
And bear imperial children in my womb
(Myself the offspring of imperial loins),
Whilst this young shootling from a baser stem
Engrosseth all the glory of his sire.

SEMP. Most gracious lady, Cæsar's leaving Gaul,
In mere obedience to his father's will,
Is but a short step towards your great design,
Though 'tis, in truth, a step.   For Constantine—
As you, indeed, complain—well loves this son,
And he, moreover, well deserves the love;
And who would take so strong a citadel—
The grave affections of a regal sire,
Built on the solid virtues of a son—

Attacks a powerful fortress, to be ta'en
Less by assault than stratagem.

FAUSTA.   And we
Must some sufficient stratagem devise.

SEMP. Ay, we must sap, by slow but sure degrees,
The rock whereon your husband's dotage stands,
That, from the failure of the base, the whole
Accumulation of his love may fall
And overwhelm his son.   Such means alone
Can compass the disgrace of the young Cæsar.
When he went forth to take command in Gaul,
Since which your gracious highness has not seen him.
He was a boy, in mind and body crude,
And his impulsive temper lacked the rein
And curb of sober thought; yet, even then,
As in the acorn sleeps the lordly oak,
There was a germ in his uncultured youth
Foretok'ning great and noble qualities.
But I have seen him in his high command,
His manhood flush, his robust thews mature,
His mind by action and experience trained,
His fitful temper by reflection poised,
And, by how much the wrought and polished gem
Exceeds in lustre the unburnished stone,
By so much doth the manhood of this prince
Outshine his youth.

FAUSTA.   Heyday, Sempronius!
These praises augur ill for my design,
Speaking of love where I would fain see hate,
And of a cold ally.   But, had he all
The virtues thou ascrib'st him fifty-fold,
Therein would seem more danger to my boys:
And therefore I'll be more resolved and stern
In my determination to undo
And break his credit with the Emperor.

SEMP. Were he mine own, your highness, I confess
I could not hold him in more just esteem,
And cannot without grief contrive him harm.
But in my breast a passion burns for you,
So fierce that near it all such trivial ties
Were frail as paltry filaments 'gainst fire.
And were he mine, and he your highness' foe,
I could regardless cast him to the wind;
For, as the mill takes motion from the stream,
My acts are prompted by your potent will.

FAUSTA. Of this no more, for here the treacherous air
May not be trusted with such dangerous words,
How faintly breathed soe'er. Of this not now,
But of the means to pluck my husband's love
From out the clod where now it firmly grows,
And plant it where I wish. This must be done;
And yet, Sempronius, 'tis no easy task.
The more one hinteth reasons for distrust,
I do believe his faith the stronger grows.

SEMP. Do not assail the son with open blame,
For so upon the father's arc of love
You shall but lay solidifying weight,
And wedge it into strength. 'Tis from below
Must come the stroke that drives the keystone forth
And leaves the arch to fall. There is a spark
I have observed oft in the Emperor's mind
Which, blown upon too roughly, will expire,
But, skilfully and gently breathed upon,
Will grow to inextinguishable flame.
That little spark is jealousy of Crispus;
For since his gallant conduct on the sea,
Which led directly to Licinius' fall,
The world has loud and louder grown in praise
Of the young Cæsar's valour. As the sun,
While he deigns shine, will not endure the stars,

Great Constantine will brook no rivalship.
And, since the reputation of his son
Hath grown so huge and caught such great applause,
Half-hidden envy and faint-gleaming spleen
Do, by impatient gestures, show themselves
In Constantine whene'er the praise is high.
If on this loose and untuned string we play,
We shall produce the discord you desire.

FAUSTA. These are the very means.   Let Constantine
Once apprehend that he affects the throne,
And all the world could not advance him further.
That over-topping and imperious will
'Fore which Maximian and Licinius fell
Shall break young Crispus too.   We'll touch this chord
Until it jars his patience.   That achieved,
Leave we the rest to him—to tune or break it.

SEMP. Be you not seen in this.   You best will serve
Your cause of hate by seeming to applaud.
Join in the admiration of the Cæsar,
Be you as loud as loudest in his praise,
And unto me and those I work through leave
The nursing of the Emperor's jealousy.
By covert hints, obscurely dropt, we will
Insinuate suspicion that this boy
(Of his affections' treasure the first gem),
Borne on the full tide of the people's praise,
Strikes for the bank of power, and turns his eyes
With premature ambition toward the throne.
When we, by crafty and insidious play,
Into the nectar of paternal love
Have, drop by drop, infused the gall of fear –
What then ?   He'll dash the tankard to the ground.

FAUSTA. So shall my hopes progress.   Let by no chance
To fan this spark of envy into hate.
I must away to Constantine; but when

I have beheld this prodigy, again
We will confer; and until then, farewell. *(Offers her
hand, which Sempronius kisses.)*   [*Exit* FAUSTA.

SEMP. Fairest but falsest woman, fare thee well.
Thou art at once my sunshine and my cloud.
Hadst thou not been, or had a trackless sea
Raged 'twixt thy beauty and my honesty,
My path had not through crooked mazes lain,
But on the broad and open walks of honour,
A pleasant journey leading to repose.
This might have been—I fear to think what may be.
Why of this woman am I still the slave,
Against my better conscience?   Well I know
That she hath vices which my heart abhors—
Hypocrisy and falseness that I hate
With the concentred loathings of my soul,
And yet which I, too, practice in her aid.
But O, my captive soul, what outward charms
Gild o'er and beautify the rot within!
The gaudy husk conceals the cankered kern.
O, that she had not been, or I were blind!—
Nay, deaf as well, for being blind, yet hearing,
Were no defence against her conquering wiles.
'Tis more for music that we love the lute
Than for its beauty.   O, melodious fiend,
Thou'st put my honour into golden gyves,
Thou'st leashed my manhood with a gilded thong,
And my volition, like a leaméd cur,
Thou leadest where thou wilt.
Enter CONSTANTINE, *his three* YOUNGER SONS, FAUSTA, OLD
HELENA, BASILIUS, &c. &c.

CON. Old Time, who flies too swiftly for our fears,
Loveth to lag and loiter to our hopes.
To my expectant eagerness, each hour
To-day hath been more tedious than a year.

O, Fausta, Fausta!   [*Shouting in the distance.*

    FAUSTA.   Hark you! Do you hear?
Those shouts, my lord, I take for warranty
That little further need your hopes be strained;
For in that distant inarticulate noise
My fancy hears the well-belovéd name
Of Crispus.

        [*More shouting and distant flourish of trumpets.*
    CON.   'Tis—it must be so.   Those trumps
Blow forth a gladsome greeting from the walls.
Now from the palace let the trumpeters
Send out a joyous note.   [*Flourish of trumpets.*
        Nay, louder still,
Till the reverberant air shall shake the ground.
Make welcome shriek from out your brazen tubes,
And turn your chests in a triumphant blast.
Blow, blow, brave trumpeters.

        [*Loud flourish of trumpets.*
        Ay, bravely done.
Anticipation in one yearning thought
Knits up existence, and all else is naught.
Delay can joyful expectations crowd
(As with the sunbeams doth a burning-glass)
Into a centre so acute and keen
That brightest prospects will occasion pain.

    FAUSTA. Do not forget, my lord, you have a wife
And other children.   I partake your joy
In the arrival of your noble son,
And love him as my own ; but I would fain
Reserve a corner in your royal heart
To keep my own love warm.

    CON.   My gentle wife,
I wrong not thee because I love my son;
And—but that absence leaves a vacant place
Here at the banquet of my boundless love,

Which I would fain have filled—he is to me
No more than those dear boys thou barest me.
For my sake, Fausta, love my gallant son.
Thou must; thou dost—or else thou lov'st not me.

    FAUSTA. What you love, I love; what you hate, so I.
I hold your house a casket of rich jewels—
A fragrant flower, of many leaves composed,
Each one its portion to the general fund
Of precious sweets imparting.

    CON.   By my life,
I made a conquest, when I took thy love,
Greater than all the triumphs of my arms.
If pleasure smiles, or if misfortune frowns,
Thy richness meets my need, for thou canst find,
For gladness, mirth—for melancholy, tears.

    FAUSTA. My breast is but a mirror to your own,
Wherein your own is doubled. When in yours
The lamp of pleasure burns, it glows in mine;
When sorrow shadeth yours, mine gloometh too.
                [*Shouting and trumpets, nearer.*

    SEMP. My liege, your son is at the palace gate.
I see the gallant prince.   [*More shouting.*
        FAUSTA *goes to window.*

    FAUSTA.   'Tis true, my lord.
Here from the casement I do see the prince
Enter the palace. I had known him not,
So much the man excels the awkward youth
That I remember Crispus; but 'tis he,
For all the crowd did bend their eyes on him,
And waved their hands and kissed their finger tips.
Now Constantine, let loose your pent-up love
And open heart and arms. Your son is here.
       Enter CRISPUS, *who embraces his father.*

    CRIS. Hail, thou old warrior! Let my arms enfold
And press thy reverend body to my breast.

Ne'er did enfranchised prisoner, from dark cell,
Rush with more rapture into light and air
Than I from pining absence to thy love.

    Con. Here let our hearts enmingle, warlike son!
O, ne'er was healing balsam to a sore
More welcome than thy presence to my soul!
Again, again, brave youth—one more embrace!
But I must not be greedy in my joy,
And eat up all thy love, for round thee stand
Thy younger brothers and their royal dam,
My aged mother, relatives, and friends
As near in love although unlinked in blood,
Whose anxious hearts are hungering to caress.

    Cris. Good friends and kin, I greet you, one and all,
And with my leisure shall my courtesy
Be more explicit and distinct to each.
But you, my grandam—venerable root,
Whence sprung the trunk of the imperial tree
Whereof my glory is to be a bough—
Here on the instant take your rightful due.   [*Kissing.*
And you, my brothers, o'er whose happy days
Time runs too swiftly (though to your bright hopes
And young ambition he may creep too slowly),
Let me embrace you all, and kiss your cheeks
While their soft skins bear no forbidding beards,
For 'twill not long be so—they'll come anon.
                 [*Kisses each of his brothers.*
Then, my fair stepdame, let me greet you too.
I blush to call you mother, for your face
Records less age then mine. Far easier 'twere
To me to call you sister. Time refrains
To blow his blighting breath upon your bloom,
But breathes aside to wither aught save you.
I am less tender. I perforce must kiss you,
For this fair brow is loadstone to these lips.   [*Kissing.*

My heart is glad to see you look so well,
And gladness o'ersteps duty; but I pray
You will forgive this childish gallantry.

FAUSTA. Where no offence, 'tis needless to forgive.
Thou'rt welcome, royal youth—thrice welcome home.
Though not thy mother, from my heart I greet thee
With more than mother's welcome.

CRIS.   This my thanks,
And count me always your devoted friend.

[*Kisses her hand.*

CON. I do rejoice that your affections thus
O'erleap the gap of birth, and cleave together
As 'twere with bent of nature.   Come, my son,
I would in private speak with thee of Gaul
Some idle moments till the feast is laid.
Go, dearest Fausta—hie thee to our guests,
And from the joy that in thine own breast burns
Distribute gladness unto all our friends.
Nor shalt thou lose by what thou dost bestow;
For 'tis the wondrous property of joy
That we may give it, yet not lose 't ourselves,
As may one lamp a thousand others light,
Yet never bate its brightness by one ray.

FAUSTA (*aside*). O, fascinating youth! I am undone
Where I was most determined to undo.
The snake that nursed her venom for his veins
Is spellbound by the music of his tongue.

[*Exeunt all but* CONSTANTINE *and* CRISPUS.

CON. My noble son, my bosom rings with joy,
But through its merry music winds a strain,
Like the soft breathing of Æolus o'er
His melancholy harp, that gently tells
How joy—like boist'rous laughter pushed to tears—
May blend with sadness or extend to pain.
Though I am pleased to see thy young form grown

Into the ripe and perfect man thou art,
And, like an oakling spreading to the sun,
Thy proud young spirit opening out to fame,
The contemplation of thy happy age
Doth from my mental eyeball lift the scale
And crust of thirty years.   Then flows a tide
Of early memories over later days,
Whose limpid waters glass me as I was
When I was young as thou; but straight it ebbs,
And shows the worn and battered thing I am,
Wherein, my son, my melancholy lies.
But I must cast it off.   What must be borne,
If borne with patience, will the easier seem,
For patience acts as cushion to a load.
There is no turning on the road of life,
And I would plod contented to the end,
How dark soe'er it be.

    CRIS.   My kingly sire,
Thy end shall be—and Providence defer
That final honour to a distant hour—
Like to a heavenly setting of the sun,
When all the glories of the summer sky
Crowd to the west to dignify his fall.

    CON. Thy speech, my son, is solace to my soul,
Proving how rich I am in thy good love.
There is to me sad sweetness in the thought
That when my old and weary bones lay down,
In silent death, the honours that I bear,
I shall behind me leave a gallant son
To take them up and wear them worthily.
Yet, when thou dost possess them, thou shalt find
Not all the honours heaped upon my age
Are worth the dreamy visions of thy youth.
Yet, what they are, they one day will be thine,
And tender tears are all the meed thou'lt owe

To him that won them for thee.   Let me see—
Nay, pardon, let me look into thine eyes.
O, could my vision peer into thy soul,
My jealous love shall probe thee all so far.
Did I suspect a rival in my crown—
That thy heart-longing could o'erlook my love
To gape for that, I had as lief have been
The poorest groom that does thee menial service.
Did I but fear thy brain could house a thought
That 'twixt my dignities and thy desires
The curtain of my life might hang too long,
'Twould be a grief—a crushing grief indeed.

   CRIS. O, father, father! were my heart not filled
With filial duty and obedient love,
Whereto irreverent anger, like a flame
To water, cometh only to expire,
These unkind thoughts had kindled me to rage.
These doubts you thrust into my breast like thorns,
Which sting the keener for a fondling hand
Doth gore me with them, and dejection comes
Where indignation may not.   Save you, sir!
As I do hope for heaven, yet fear to die,
The prospect of your death doth more appal
My apprehension than your honours, told
A thousand-fold, could e'er affect my hopes.
If I have youth that may endure fatigue,
If courage that may serve you in your wars,
If sense or skill to guide your helm in peace,
If truth that may be faithful to your trust,
If life or limb to prop your dignity,
I to your service frankly tender all,
And humbly do beseech your use of them,
That care may sit more lightly on your life.
Make of my youth a cushion to your age,
Whereon your wisdom may in ease recline,

In the full splendour of your majesty.

Con. I do believe thee—on my life, I do—
And heavily will draw upon thy love.

Cris. The treasure shall not fail you in your need.

Con. Forgive my humour, for I thought aloud
Rather than spoke to thee. No, Crispus, no;
I would not wound thy young and generous heart
For all the wealth within my sceptre's sway;
But I have passed that pitch upon life's round
Wherefrom the wheel doth fall, and baseless fears
Are to that period all as apt and prone
As airy hopes and castles to the young.
Come to my closet; then we'll to the feast. [*Exeunt.*

SCENE 2.—Another Part of the Palace.

Enter Pappus *and* Benevolentius, *at opposite sides.*

Ben. Good even, Pappus. Well, what dost thou think
of the Cæsar now? Thou didst know him as a boy, and
having to-day journeyed some distance in his company,
and had, withal, discourse with him, thou knowest him
now as a man. What dost thou think of him?

Pap. Think of him! I have no words to tell thee what
I think of him. This is the happiest day of my life. I
never fell out with my grey hairs till I saw the Cæsar in
his manhood. Heretofore I have regarded them as the
insignia of wisdom, and infinitely more honourable than
the gaudy flaunting locks that make the fopling proud; but
the young Crispus—Heaven bless him!—with the beauty
and vigour that become his years, has the wisdom of a
sage; and his judgment so sparkles on his good looks that
they seem to be its natural foil. Since I have seen him I
have come to despise this thin white fleece of mine, which
seems rather to symbolise poverty and pallor in my wits
than to be any token of my wisdom.

Ben. He is, indeed, a most wise young prince; and the

more thou seest of him the more thou shalt be convinced of his judgment.

PAP. Ay, he is somewhat wise; there's no gainsaying that; and yet I was less struck with his judgment than his beauty.

BEN. I took thee to say just now that thou wast most struck with his wisdom.

PAP. Heyday, young man! Hast thou no more grace than to contradict thy elders.

BEN. Why, didst thou not say that his wit flashed from his beauty like a jewel from its setting?

PAP. No, coxcomb, I—that is, only to an extent, only to an extent. I said he was wise for his years, and I say so still; but no man is wise at his years, and, upon reflection, I have known younger men wiser than he. But for good looks, I grant thee he is the masterpiece of creation.

BEN. Is he not, Pappus? Didst thou ever see such eyes? May not one see honesty in them?

PAP. Certainly, he has a fine eye; yet it is something vacant, and its vacancy looks like honesty.

BEN. But his hair, Pappus! Might not his locks adorn the temples of Apollo?

PAP. Well, undoubtedly, his locks are ample, and withal somewhat flowing; and yet his hair is too coarse to be pleasing.

BEN. Coarse, Pappus? Why, 'tis fine as floss.

PAP. Pray respect thy seniors, young man. I say his hair is coarse—coarse as well-ropes. It is the chief blemish of his beauty.

BEN. Well, Pappus, I will not anger thee by contradiction. I will give in to thy humour about the hair; but what canst thou say against the dignity and grace of his features?

PAP. Nothing, indeed, against his features.

BEN. Is he not handsome beyond all else thou hast ever
beheld ?

PAP. No; by no means.   He is passably well-looking; •
but his beauty is only borrowed, for he had it from his
father, who is better looking than he.

BEN. Yet he is handsome.   Then, the straightness of his
limbs, the proportioned breadth of his shoulders, the fulness of his chest, the curve of his loins, the strength of
his haunches, the poise of his head, the spring and firm-
ness of his gait— By my life, he is the perfection of
manhood.

PAP. Hold to thy own opinions, young man; by all
means, judge for thyself.   But let me tell thee that the
poverty of thy taste is proof of the folly of thy years.

BEN. Why, thou old crabstock, thou art more shifty
than the wind.

PAP. Thou liest, insolent coxcomb.   I stick to what I
said at first: he is wry-necked.

BEN. Thou liest, dotard.

PAP. He is squint-eyed.

BEN. Thou liest.

PAP. He is round-shouldered, low-chested, calf-mouthed,
weak-loined, flat-footed, and I'll wager, when his legs are
seen, he is either bandy-legged or buck-shinned.

BEN. Thou liest, thou liest, thou liest.

PAP. He is the ugliest man, save thee, I ever had the
ill fortune to set eyes upon, and the greatest dunce in the
Roman empire.

BEN. He is the handsomest being below the gods, and
the most honourable Roman living.

PAP. Go mend thy manners and thy judgment, princox.
I leave thee with contempt.   [Exit.

BEN. Nay, thou leavest me rather without contempt, for
thou bearest mine with thee.   If I wish to be friendly
with Pappus, it will never do to agree with him.   [Exit.

SCENE 3.—A Banquet in the Palace.

CONSTANTINE, CRISPUS, FAUSTA, SEMPRONIUS, &c. &c. *with*
Courtiers, Ladies, and Attendants, discovered.

CON. Since all are satisfied, and tempting viands
Prick not our jaded appetites to more
(Our fulness loathing what our hunger craved),
As from the feast you rise, a general pledge
We drink, of health and long life unto all.
Now to your revels, for we waive all form,
That ceremony's slow and stately wain
Encumber not, with tedious pace, the ground
Whereon fleet-footed pleasure pants to run.

SEMP. I would beseech a minute's pause, my liege.
Three gentlemen, deputed by the town
That duty to discharge, entreat your leave
To read and to present a short address,
Congratulating—

CON.   This is badly timed.

SEMP. It is, my lord, and so I argued them ;
But they persist, confiding in the love
That spurs the error to condone the fault.
To their good hope I add my humble prayer.

CON. We'll hear it read, but with all decent speed,
For what pertains to us we well could waive.

SEMP. (*aside to Fausta.*) This is a hash of vain and
        fulsome praise,
Which might upon the grossest stomach pall ;
But in't is reference that will his grudge
Against the Cæsar—now an itching spot,
Unseen till rubbed—yet chafe into a sore,
And which, once fretted raw, must never heal.

Three DEPUTIES *advance, and bend before* CONSTANTINE.

1ST DEP. (*reading*). Illustrious Constantine, of monarchs
        prime,
The first and mightiest soldier of the world,

In peace as wise as obstinate in war,
Before whose fame the burning wreaths that glow
Round ancient heroes' temples fade and wane,
Like paltry night-lamps in the sheen of day,—
With trembling homage we approach your throne,
Our lives and duties at your feet to lay.
Great conqueror, behold our prostrate forms,
Unto your princely feet a humble stool,
To lift your wisdom nearer to the clouds
Whence first it emanated, and whereto
It one day must—sad fate for earth!—return.

    Cris. (*aside*). Can this vile flattery and these abject
        slaves
Have sprung from noble Rome?   Faugh! 'tis most foul.
Then art thou dead indeed, majestic Rome,
For carrion only could such vermin breed.
So maggots thrive when dignity decays.

    Con. (*aside*). He frowns, as in disgust, and turns away.
His dainty stomach finds the food too gross.
So, so—their praises please him not.   Well, well.

    1st Dep. We come catch some stray drops of the joy
That from your heart abundantly runs o'er,
And humbly crave to welcome the return
From distant dangers of your warrior son,
That brave, that virtuous, and that beauteous prince,
Who from your own sublimity proceeds
As dazzling lustre issues from the sun.

    Con. (*aside*). He is the lustre, then, and I the sun.
So I, the sun, of my own light bereaved,
Remain but ashes from the Cæsar's fire.

    Cris. (*smiling contemptuously*). Disgusting trash!

    Con. (*aside*). So, so—thou smilest now.
Thyself the theme, their adulation seems
Less grossly nauseous, does it?   Good.   Go to.

    1st Dep. We greet thee, mighty son of mighty sire!

We glorify thy brilliant feats of arms,
And specially that naval triumph name,
Gained o'er Licinius in the Hellespont,
Which gave the purple of thy worthy sire
A richer hue and more capacious—

  CON.   Hold!
I do beseech you, moderate your praise.
Let commendation halt whilst further still,
Without o'ermarching merit, it may go;
For praise should wait on worthiness, and walk.
Like an attendant, somewhat in the rear,
When praise outweighs the virtues we commend,
We raise a column on too frail a base,
That crumbles 'neath the weight 'tis sought to bear.
Like decoration pushed to glittering gawd,
That which we would enrich we only mar.
Come, come, you weary me—I'll hear no more.
The night wears fast—your scroll is much too long.
Go—get you gone!   Let pleasure now succeed
This dreary adulation.   Go, go, go.   [*Exeunt* DEPUTIES.

  CRIS. I do not marvel that your patience wears.
When I succeed to your unbounded power—
If e'er I do, and distant be the day—
When such lip-serving sycophants as these
Would blow their fulsome incense face,
I'll have the slaves lashed hound-like from the court.

  CON. (*aside*). Does not this mean I am a vain old
    man ?
" When I succeed," eh ?   I have other sons.
I love thee, lad; but thou art over bold.
I must a while retire, good gentle friends.
I am not well; a dull and heavy pain
Hath shot athwart and throbs within my brow ;—
I need some short repose.   Be not concerned :
I'll be myself anon, and come again.

CRIS. O, sovereign father, this is sad indeed!
You are the very girdle of the fête,
The union-link that runs through all our hearts,
The silken string that binds our bunch of flowers;
And you, alas, unwell! Your illness, sire,
Will snap the cord, and scatter the bouquet.
   CON. May health, like dews from kindly heaven,
      descend
Upon thy head, and keep thee young for aye.
I am already almost whole again.
On with the dance, and think no more of me.
I will be with you straight; I'm better now.
My filthy fears are traitors to my peace (aside).
Henceforth I'll listen to my heart alone,
Which tells me he is true.   [Exit.
   SEMP. (aside to Fausta). The poison works,
And, though the antidote appears to sooth,
Its venom yet shall sink into the soul.   [Exit.
   FAUSTA (aside). Alas, alas! how guiltiness recoils
On those that use it! Who by evil works
Doth up an incline push a ponderous stone,
Which, when his force is spent, rolls back on him.
The fiend I've raised to scare the Cæsar's quiet
Frights my own peace. I fear my own ally.
A Dance, after which the Company gradually disperse.
   CRIS. What is your age, good mother?
   FAUSTA.   Now too old
To own it frankly had I not been wed.
O, fie on thee, to ask a lady's age!
When once a woman passes twenty-five,
Her age becomes a secret, to be guessed,
Not bluntly asked; and courtesy should err
Upon the side of youth in guessing it.
   CRIS. Nay, pardon me. Indeed, I meant no harm.
I'd rather die than wittingly be rude;

But you in air and person look so well,
So rich in beauty, and withal so young,
That I do marvel how your charms outwear
The nurture of your family.   E'en I
(On whom the hand of time hath busier been)
Should name you mother; yet, regarding age,
It seemeth mockery to call you so.

    FAUSTA. And, Crispus, well it may, for o'er my head
So many summers have not shed their suns
But I might be thy sister.   Nay, I've known
(The woman, too, the elder of the twain)
'Twixt man and wife more difference of years
Than is 'twixt thine and mine—and even then
No great disparity.   When Constantine
Did woo and wed me, I was scarce fifteen ;
And ere another year had passed away,
Thy brother, young Constantius, saw the world.
Thou art his elder by at least ten years ;
So that six winters—scarcely more than five—
Are all the burthen that my shoulders bear
Of age more than thine own.

    CRIS.   Why, that is nothing.
When I was younger, you did older seem.
The boy's eye sees things greater than the man's.
A coming year in childhood longer seems
Than do ten spent ones to the upgrown man ;
So hope doth lengthen and regret curtail
The course of time.
This life is but the clamber of a hill.
We labour upward, longing for the top,
Which gained, we for a little space look round,
Then timidly the other side descend;
And all our pains are to go gently down,
And, by avoiding footslip, save a fall.

    FAUSTA. So sadly sage, and yet but twenty-three?

Thou speakest more like three score years than one.
Thy mind seems cast in melancholy's mould;
Thou think'st too deeply.   Wherefore brood so much?
The thoughtless are the blithest in this world.

    Cris. Ay, true; I'm merriest when I think the least.
But pleasure seldom bideth long in me;
For when I am most filled with careless joy,
Reflection, like a leakage in the mind,
Drains all away to dreary emptiness.

    Fausta. I dare be sworn thou art in love, then.
    Cris. No,
Save with myself and cold philosophy.

    Fausta. Art thou so cold that nature chills in thee?
Is woman's beauty nothing to thine eye?
Is thy heart stone?
    Cris.   As frail as any man's,
As nervous to the touch of loveliness,
And of an eyelash oft hath felt the wales.
But of that loftier and more holy flame,
Which is the growth of time and constancy—
When intercourse and tried companionship
Have warmed light lovers into stable friends—
I have no knowledge save by hearsay yet.

    Fausta. Didst never love?
    Cris.   Yea, when I was a boy,
I loved a little maid, and she loved me—
Or so, at least, we said, and thought so then—
And we did plight our baby troth, and vowed
That each one in the other's heart should dwell.
It was a childish freak, and lightly done
As scholars writing "love" upon their slates.
Sad things have chanced since then; and busy Time,
Using my silent absence as a sponge,
Hath doubtless wiped the record from her brain.
I mind it well; and yet the circumstance

Lives rather in my memory than my heart.
I see her image now.   But tell me, tell me—
Is not Helena here about the court ?
    FAUSTA. She is.
    CRIS.   Then why does she so long withhold
The blessing of her welcome ?   Is she ill ?
    FAUSTA. She is not well ; indeed, 'tis many days—
Some five or six now—since she left her chamber.
Yet she did promise, when the feast was o'er,
To grace your welcome by her presence here.
Look where, with wan and thoughtful face, she comes.
    CRIS. Pale, truth, she is, but bright as the chaste moon,
Looking, by contrast with her tending maids.
Like Phœbe as she glides before the stars.
She sees me now, and as she smiles she warms ;
Her gentle blood runs blushing to her cheeks,
As if her heart hung out a crimson flag
To welcome me.   This was my early love.
Sure she's an angel! for the gap between
Her peerless beauty and all womankind
Is all as wide and spacious as the void
'Twixt heaven and earth.
    FAUSTA (aside).   May blight and pestilence
Strike down her health and rot her loathsome charms.
                Enter HELENA.
    HEL. My memory knows thee not, but there's my
            hand,
And in it grasp the welcome of my heart.
Tell not thy name, for, swifter to mine eye
Than could thy tongue proclaim it to mine ear,
Thy face tells who thou art.   The noble die
That stamped distinction on thy mighty sire
Hath set the seal of dignity on thee ;
But on thy youth it looks more round and full.
For upon him the heavy hand of age

Hath pressed a deeper print.   Thou'rt welcome, cousin.

   Cris. 'Tis with my welcome e'en as with the feast,
The daintiest dish comes last.   Bewitching girl,   •
Though thy good greeting fills me with delight,
Thou hast not sated—nay, nor satisfied.
One craving gorged, another empty gapes ;
And, like a greedy and a thievish boor,
Who from a golden vessel slakes his thirst,
And covets then the cup, so I, fair cousin,
Now that I've quaffed the welcome of thy heart,
Would steal the heart itself.   To save the crime,
Bright wonder, give it me.

    Hel.   What, give my heart,
And leave my bosom empty ?

    Cris.   Nay, take mine
To fill the void.   I will exchange with thee.

    Hel. But is it worth the having ?

    Cris.   It is sound
And whole as adamant.

    Hel.   Perchance as hard,

    Cris. As precious 'tis, but tender as the grape ;
And as a grape matureth in the sun,
So in thy smiles my heart hath grown so full
With ripeness, that 'tis falling from the tree.
Prithee spread forth the apron of thy love,
And catch it ere it drops into the mire.

    Hel. Thou'rt merry, cousin—ha, ha, ha!

    Fausta.   Ha, ha!
Beware, Helena, if you prize your peace,
How you believe this flatterer.   Just now
He said he knew not what it was to love,
Albeit he owned that beauty had a spell
That oft o'ermastered him.   Ha, ha !   Beware !
He is a roving lover, like the bee.

    Cris. Nay, nay, you twist my meaning, gentle mother.

FAUSTA (*aside*). Sdeath! is it mother now? So soon
     grown old?

CRIS. I did confess myself as sensitive
To loveliness as all male mortals are,
And still declared that yet I had not loved.
That soul is dead that beauty fails to charm.
A noble picture pleases us, a rose,
A well-cut statue, or a melody;
Yet are there many paintings, various flowers,
Abundant sculptures, and as numerous airs,
Which have the power to charm as much or more.
Such feeling smacks of wonder more than love.
True love must look for beauty in the soul;
For sympathy, the vestal fire of love,
That pure flame which, when beauty breaks and fades—
When time hath sucked the lustre from the eye,
Picked from the mouth its cherries, stolen its pearls,
Withered youth's roses, whitened every hair,
And where the roses grew deep furrows ploughed—
Will burn to cheer the ruin as the prime.
But if I knew not how to love this morn,
I've ta'en, at least, a potent lesson now.
Those letters that compose Helena's name
Shall be to me the alphabet of love,
And, like a patient student failing aid,
I'll plod till I am master of the art,
Save my fair cousin will abridge my pains
By kindly tutoring.

HEL.   I know thee now.
I marvel that I knew thee not at once.

CRIS. And yet you smiled upon me as you came,
And without telling—

HEL.   Guessed who thou shouldst be,
From where thou art, thy bearing, being strange,
And thy resemblance to the Emperor,

Not from my recollection of thyself.
But with thy voice each feature on me stole,
As music oft recalls forgotten words;
And now my memory is distinct and clear
As if we had grown up together.   Ah!
I well remember, when we parted, words
More serious than these present levities.

   CRIS. Dost thou remember, then, those fervent words
When we were children?

   HEL.   Better than thy face.
But how hast thou remembered them?

   CRIS.   As well
E'en as thyself, and will repeat them now.

   HEL. But ere thou dost expect me to believe,
Vouchsafe some bond for constancy.

Enter SEMPRONIUS.

   SEMP.   My lord,
The Emperor is again astir, and calls
Impatiently for you.

   CRIS.   Nor calls in vain.
I will attend him instantly.   Come, cousin;
Give me thy hand for partner in the dance.
Let time and use confirm thy wavering faith,
For like the amaranth my love has blown,
Its bloom to be immortal.   Come, sweet girl!

[Exeunt CRISPUS and HELENA.

   FAUSTA. Thou pale faced minion, what sees he in thee?
Secure in my own beauty, until now
I've looked upon thee as a pretty babe,
To fondle, not to fear.   Yet now, I find
Thou canst attract where I am fain to cling.
If't be thy look of milky innocence,
I'll be the cat to lap it out of thee.

SEMPRONIUS comes forward.

   SEMP. May I be bold to ask why you so frowned

When they went forth together ?

FAUSTA.   Did I frown ?

SEMP. In truth you did, as though destruction would,
Did power but second will, have blasted her.

FAUSTA. I like her not.

SEMP.   And why ?

FAUSTA.   Dull stupid churl,
Canst thou not see, that if he marry Helen
He will thereby Licinius' faction gain,
And, if a son should from the union spring,
The Emperor's favour, which we shift from him,
Might settle on that son. If so it fell,
Where were the wished advantage to my own ?

SEMP. These reasons have, in truth, a certain force.

FAUSTA. This sad result to obviate, you must
With me contrive, ere they can cream their love,
To sour it into hate.

SEMP.   I am content,
That end to thwart, to lend you every aid,

FAUSTA. My husband's mother is approaching. Quick!
Away at once, for she suspects—

SEMP.   Farewell.   [*Exit.*

         OLD HELENA *crosses stage.*

FAUSTA. O, what a wretched guilty thing I feel!
That I, the father's wife, should love the son !
'Tis monstrous—foul. Why should I love the father ?
Have I not rather cause for mortal hate ?
Did he not kill my father and my brother ?
Was I not led, when yet a timid girl,
A youthful offering to his lustful prime,
To patch a faithless peace betwixt the two—
My husband and my father—hollow truce,
That ended in the old man's butchery ?
And hath my husband counted not in years
Enough to be my father? Say, my heart,

What love can I, on such compulsion, owe?
Why, none at all; nor any will I pay—
Nor e'er have paid, save what hypocrisy
Hath for my profit and my safety feigned.
Will not the crookless sword of tempered steel,
The pressure ta'en away when bent and strained,
Resume its former straightness?   So will I,
Though in the spring I cut the tyrant hand
That's held me crook'd so long.   I was betrothed
Unto this man Sempronius ere my marriage;
But in the garden of my heart the seed
Of his exotic passion would not root.
O, Crispus, Crispus! thou'rt the only man
With whom my fierce love ever tried a throw,
And every chance against me.   Decency,
Morality, religion, nature's self,
Have put between us an eternal bar.
Yet, could I win thy love, I'd sweep them all,
Like reeds, from 'twixt my passion and my joy.

                                        [Exit.

ACT II.

SCENE 1.—Nicomedia.   A Room in the Palace.
CONSTANTINE *discovered.*

CON. Why am I not most happy, when I sit
High as my envy reached, and far beyond
My wildest primal hopes ?   Why not content,
When, like an eagle, I have soared so high,
And perch upon the apex of the world ?
My sovereign arm can wield my sceptre o'er
The civil earth, and in the dust strike down
What I dislike, or raise whate'er I love.
Who climbs a mountain to be near the sun,
Hoping for warmth, must bear the bitter blast.
So in my lofty grandeur do I find
Sad isolation—frosty solitude ;
And there are times when I would fain descend
To the companionships of humbler days.
Alas, it cannot be !
The wings on which I soared have not the power
To bear me safely down, would I descend.
We mount by steps to greatness, but, being up,
Have no descent but by a headlong fall.

Enter SEMPRONIUS.

How goes the day, Sempronius ?

SEMP.   Past high noon
Almost an hour.

CON.   Didst thou stay to see
The troops manœuvre ?

SEMP.   Ay, my sovereign liege.
And kept the ground till they were marched away.
I was much pleased.

CON.   I thought to see them too,
But on the ground I caught a creeping chill

That forced me to withdraw.   I am not well.

SEMP. I grieve, my lord—

CON.   What meant those boisterous shouts •
I heard an hour ago ?   Was Crispus there ?

SEMP. He was, my liege ; it was his coming thither
That called the tumult forth.   You should be proud
To see your son so high in favour grown—
So popular with the troops.

CON.   Humph.

SEMP.   Scarce he came
Till all the legions, looking with one eye,
Did recognise him ; then, as with one tongue,
Went forth the loud huzza.   Then came the buzz
And gurgling murmur of more varied cries—
As "Crispus," "Cæsar," "Gaul," "Byzantium";—
But ten "Byzantium" bawled for every one
That cried aught else.   Then such confusion followed,
As if each soldier—each particular man—
Writhed i' the leash of discipline, and fain
Would from his rapture slip the galling noose,
Fly from the ranks, and hug him to each heart.

CON. 'Twas no such greeting that they gave to me.
Me they saluted with the cold precision
And formal readiness that grows from use,
Not with enthusiasm.   Their huzzas
Were but as lazy hummings to a cue,
Heavy and drowsy as the drawling chaunt
Of "Amen" in a church.

SEMP.   I did observe.

CON. What was his victory on Licinius' fleet
Against Byzantium ?   The very stage—
The showhouse of his fame—the Hellespont
Is but a paltry artery o' the sea
I could almost bestride, and he a player
That spouts what better than himself had penned :—

For he did only what myself had planned,
And I have mean subalterns in my pay
Had done't as well as he. I am amazed
A deed so small should such a tumult rouse,
And that the windy mouth of servile praise
Should, from a cup of such poor soapy froth,
Have blown a bubble that fills all the world.
But, by my crown, I'll prick it and disperse't.

   SEMP. The time and the conditions make a deed
Or great and noted, or contemptible ;
For, in the calm and stillness of the night,
Weak noise cracks loud, and small sounds swell the air,
Travel afar, and reach to distant ears,
Which in the buzz and bustle of the day
Would not be noted. You must oft have seen
That when the wind is still, the water smooth,
A little pebble cast into a mere
Sends o'er its glassy breast a rippling ring
That strikes on every shore, when, had the breeze
Over the bosom of the water blown,
It merely would have splashed, and there an end.
So show the petty conquests of your son.
The turmoil of your life is o'er, my liege :
Your glory glitters in the calm of eve ;
Your name shines in the firmament of fame
The brightest of its stars. Long seen and known,
Your aye-enduring lustre is a thing
Familiar to the eye, not wondered at ;
Whilst he, a meteor shooting o'er the sky,
Is for the moment more observed than you.

   CON. No, no, Sempronius, no, it is not so :
I know 'tis different. The flimsy veil
Which thy good love and my poor spleen cast o'er
His martial merit hideth not his fame.
Though I did plan, yet did he execute

As from my hand it fell.   I had a dream.

BAS. A dream?

ALL.   A dream?

MAN.   O, let us hear thy dream.

Enter a Servant, bowing.

CRIS. Bring wine and goblets. Quick. [*Exit Servant.*

BAS.   Come, come—the dream.

CRIS. I'll tell you that anon.   This supple slave
Most painfully reminds me of my dream.
We'll have a soldier for our cupbearer.

Re-enter Servant, with wine, &c.

Benevolentius shall attend us here.
Tell him I want him.   So—thou canst withdraw.

[*Exit Servant.*

BAS. I drink to Crispus. (*Drinks.*)

ALL (*drinking*).   Crispus.

CRIS.   Thanks, my friends.

Enter BENEVOLENTIUS.

Thou art a soldier, friend, whose arm in Gaul
Hath done me service. Is't below thy pride
To fill the cups and hand about the wine?

BEN. O, no, my lord.   I'll do it with the best will in the
world; but I care not to have my office confined to the
filling of the cups, for you will find me just as handy at
the emptying of them.

CRIS. O, thou shalt drink thy fill.   Thou shalt be to as
a semi-equal for the time, and I trust to thy soldierly dis-
cretion not to overstep the bounds of modest privilege. I
care not to have this limber knave about my person.

BEN. I know my place, my lord.   But touching this
limp-backed lackey, an he come into the room again, if
your lordship will but give me leave to kick him out of
it, it would be a great comfort to my toes.

CRIS. If he return I may think of thy good offices.

BAS. Come, noble Crispus, you forget your dream.

Cris. First let me drink. My throat and tongue
    are dry,
Parched and distempered with a burning thirst.
    (Benevolentius *serves wine.*)
And now my dream. Attend me well. Methought
Beneath an elm tree's grateful shade I lay,
To shelter from a scorching noonday sun,
Upon a bank whose green and velvet turf
Sloped gently to a clear and gurgling rill;
When by there came a pretty rustic maid,
In cloak and hood, with basket on her arm.
She smiled askantly as she passed me by;
Anon, with hesitation in her step,
She halted, and upon my face she turned
The full and searching lustre of her eyes.
Then from her basket in her plump white hand
Two eggs she took, and said, " Sir, will you buy ?"
" If that your wares be fresh as your bright eyes,
I'll buy them," I replied. " Then, sir, behold !"
She sweetly said, and held one toward the sun.
At once, methought, the sun became a cloud,
And instant night and darkness filled the air.
I knew the maid then for Herophile,
As, flinging back her hood, she slowly said,
"The fruits and blossoms of a thousand suns
Have crisped and withered in a thousand snows
Since this was laid, though fresh for ever more."
Upon the shell was writ, as 'twere in fire,
" Roman Republic." Then within did glow
A light which, growing, seemed to stretch the shell
Into an airy and invisible gauze,
And on a disc of pure ethereal blue
The figures of two antique Romans showed.
The one (plain citizen, in homely gown),
As if to urge some suit with manly power,

Did grasp the other's hand persuadingly.
The stature of the second was more tall,
And had the poise, the gesture, and the mien
Of high nobility and conscious power ;
And in his toga's graceful folds there flowed,
And through the looseness of his locks there streamed,
And on the fine mould of his face there shone,
And over all there breathéd—Liberty.
These slowly melted, and the Sibyl then
Stretched forth the second egg, on which was traced,
In bloody script, "The Empire."   "This," she said,
" Though newly stolen from the nest of Fate,
Is foul within and rotten to its core."
Then, as before, upon a disc I saw
Three figures: one of good and manly mien,
Whose shapely form did need no ornament,·
Yet clad in gaudy many-coloured robes,
So painted, and so pencilled, and so stained.
And so bespangled and besprent with gems,
That in the sheen and pomp I lost the man.
And at his feet there crouched two cringing slaves,
Who, like two spaniels, licked the jewelled shoes.
I looked again into the face, and saw,
With heart half rived, the features of my sire.
Your friendly shake then waked me from my dream.
    SEMP. (*aside*). This dream shall cost thee thy com-
           mand in Gaul.
    MAN. This is most strange. But what may it portend ?
You will consult the augur ?
    CRIS.   Nay, not I.
'Tis but a picture of my waking thoughts
Unquiet sleep has painted on my brain.
My mind, uneasy in the present, oft
In rambling fancy wanders o'er the past,
And therefrom always turneth with regret

To look upon the future with dismay.

MAN. I too, my lord, am with such musings plagued,
But dare not speak —

CRIS. Where is your Roman now ?

MAN. Ay, where, indeed ?

CRIS. I' faith, it makes me sad.

SEMP. Benevolentius, you neglect your charge.
The prince is moody ; give his highness wine.
Come, come, my lord, drown sadness in a cup.
You, Mannius, try the virtues of the vine.
Your health, my lord. (*Drinks.*)

CRIS. (*drinking*). I drink to all.

ALL (*drinking*). The prince.

SEMP. (*aside*). They're in the humour now. But
drink enough,
And from their glib and greasy tongues will glide,
If not rank treason, what shall treason seem.

CRIS. In these degraded and degenerate times
Greatness stalks trampling o'er the populace ;
But in the rare days when old Rome was free,
Good men were lifted by the general choice
Into the high seat of authority.

MAN. Here in the glitter of the court, my lord,
Men bask in all the splendour of the sun,
While, neath the clouds whose golden sides they see,
Pine myriads upon myriads in the shade.
Thy father's eye, he sitting in the light,
Sees not into the gloom. I, in a room,
As 'twere, observe the antics of the flies
That flutter round him upon tuneful wings.
O, the sly sycophants, I know them well !
Their ceremony, form, obsequiousness,
Their lithe servility, the hum of praise
They buzz into his ear, are make-believes
That they do bear no stings ; but let him fall—

Let fail the pinions of his power, which now
Like fans protect him—and upon his face
They'll turn the venom of their painted tails,
And blister where they sing.   I know the knaves.

CRIS. It is most true; and those that readiest cringe,
Who are most supple where perforce they bend,
Are, wheresoever they may stand erect,
Most rigid in their pride.

MAN.   The maxim seems,
" Fawn where we must, and trample where we may."

CRIS. 'Tis not the worst, good Mannius, that they fawn,
But that by fawning they attain the power
To trample.   Such men round my father swarm,
Commended by their smirking limberness,
Who, having into favour smiled themselves,
Gain posts of honour and high consequence.
The humble-bending suitor of to-day
May on the morrow stiff in judgment sit.
Too many such do now give out the law,
Straining its letter to their selfish ends;
For justice, which should glow like light, and shine
All over nature, they compound and sell,
Like merchandise, to him that best can pay.
Such are like leeches on the commonwealth,
Who—not applied with the physician's skill,
To suck from fulness superfluity—
Assail the puny vessels of the poor,
Where life runs meagrely, and with the blood
They drain the health away.

MAN. I tell thee, Crispus, that these lordly drones
Spring from the ignorance of the populace,
As fungus grows on dung.   Were all men taught,
No man could rise beyond his fellows' bound
Save on the wings of merit.

CRIS.   Were all men

But wisely taught, and honest were as wise,
It might be so.   Where honour is the judge,
Worth meets its meed.   Where jealousy awards,
Subservience finds more favour than desert.

 Bas. (*aside*). Sempronius, this is treason.
 Semp.   Hold thy tongue,
Hark, and in memory store up what thou hear'st,
As something found, which time may turn to use.

 Cris. The course of Rome hath been that of a stream,
Whose waters first in sparkling clearness welled
From out the free heights of antiquity,
Which, whilst it in restricted channels ran,
Right merrily did brawl and brightly flow,
Bounds giving motion, motion purity.
But soon her saving limits did expand,
Her clearness clouding as her action slowed,
And now, as having gained a spacious plain,
She overspreads the world, and stagnant grows,
Her surface curding pestilential scum.

 Semp. The things, my lord, that make you thus
    despond,
Methinks, should furnish reasons to rejoice.
Has not your august sire, with his good sword,
Hewn down all thwarts and hindrance to his rule—
Mown, reaper-like, all covert from his throne
Wherein might coil the serpent treachery—
That he, and you, and your illustrious line,
May, from the well cleared plateau of his power,
In easy safety overlook the world ?

 Cris. And was the world made for the weal of one,
To the enslavement of the race ?   Not so,
Not so, Sempronius.   My inward eye
Can, by the great light of the Christian creed,
Read on the page of nature that the hind,
The poorest slave we mutilate and scourge,

Is in the image of his Maker formed
As much as Constantine.   I covet more
To be revered for virtue than be feared
And flattered for my power.   I do not say
That I am unambitious, but my pride
Would sit upon the shoulders of esteem,
Not stand upon the neck of abject fear.

    SEMP. He that would rule the rabble through its love,
And taketh not a tight grip on its fears,
Essays to ride unbridled a wild horse,
His seat no safer, and his course less sure.

    CRIS. By heaven, I'd rather fight afoot 'mongst men
Than ride, as on a pavement, over slaves.

    SEVERAL (*drinking*). Long live our future Emperor!
           The prince!

    BAS. (*aside to Sempronius*). This is the rankest treason.

    SEMP. Hush! Hear more.
The feathers by a moulting eagle shed
May fledge a dart to fetch him off the wing.

    BEN. (*aside*). This whispering means knavery, or I sin.

    SEMP. My noble lord, when you shall take the helm
To guide the vessel of the state through time,
You'll find the water calm.   Not so your sire;
When he assumed it, stormy were the waves,
But like old Neptune he bade them be still,
And they obeyed his genius.   He arose
Like Phœbus, in a lowering clouded sky,
And for a while 'twas doubtful and unsure
Which would prevail, the sunshine or the storm.
But he dispersed the vapours with his power,
And passed the dubious crisis of the noon
In such a full flood of resplendent fire
As did confirm the glory of his day.

    CRIS. The glitter of the empire is unreal.
Its gaudy pomp and soulless pageantry

Are but as colours on a putrid pool.
The broad-blown empire is too wide for rule.
The hand is smaller than the thing 'twould hold,
And what it fain would gripe it scarce can span.
The Emperor's majesty is fourfold mirrored
In the proud prefects, and their own again
A hundred-fold in their subordinates.
Hence numberless defections ; for the state
Is less a solid empire than a crowd
Of paltry kingdoms.   From my father's hand,
Their number being too plenteous for his grasp,
They fall away like pebbles 'twixt the fingers,
And in the taking up thrust others forth.

 SEMP. (*aside*). Can he have heard of the revolt in
  Gaul ?

 BAS. I'll hear no more. Sempronius.

 SEMP.   Stay, man, stay.

BEN. (*aside*). More whispering.   These knaves mean
mischief to the young prince, the good nature of whose
heart runs out at his tongue like wine from a cracked
bottle.   Though my head be broken for it, I'll change the
tune.   (*To Crispus.*)   What are the aims of Government,
my lord.

 CRIS. To what end askest thou ?

 BEN. That I may give you the benefit of sage advice,
and show you wherein you may amend the laws.

 BAS. Ha, ha, ha !   Presumptuous slave !

 CRIS. I think not so, Basilius, for the world
'Neath shaggy hair hath seen wise heads ere now ;
And for the humour of the hour we will
Take counsel with him.   Well, my most sage friend,
Some of the aims of government are these :
To curb the strong, and to defend the weak ;
To keep those honest who would fain be rogues
And give protection unto honest men ;

To punish vice, and virtue to reward ;
Or, in a word, to make mankind content.

BEN. To make the rogue honest, and you talk of punish-
ments. Therein you err most grievously, my lord. Why
rule through fear when you could do it better through
honour? Were I an emperor, as I should have been—a
plague on the fate that marred me—I'd have no punish-
ments, but would rule by rewards, appealing, through
their interests, to the honour of men. Only make honesty
more profitable than roguery, and you will have no
thieves.

MAN. Ha, ha, ha, ha!

BAS.   The man's an idiot.

CRIS.   Why,
What is this honour where there's no dislike
To doing right or prompting to do wrong?
'Tis in temptation, man, that honour shines,
As doth a torch or lantern in the night;
And where there is no motive to be mean,
The flaunt and brag of honour is as poor
And pitiful as candlelight at noon.

BEN. Blow candles out. I'd have no lamps, torches, or
tapers, but perpetual daylight. Appeal to a man's honour
in this wise : If a man be tempted to steal an *as*, and he
be able to prove that he resisted the prompting, let the
state award him the value of an *as* and a half ; and if all
men knew beforehand that their honesty would be thus
rewarded, there would not be a thief in Christendom.

CRIS. Ha, ha, ha! There would be more of novelty, I
fear, than of utility in thy legislation. Thou wouldst try
to cure greed with gorging.

BAS. A perfect ass. Why waste your breath, my lord,
on such a blockhead?

CRIS. If 'twere the fashion to regard vice as virtue,
and the contrary, then indeed thy method might avail.

BEN. The fashion is everything, my lord, for an act may be either a vice or a virtue, as it is the fashion to regard it. The virtues of one generation may be the vices of the next. What with the Spartans was a virtue would be a scandal among the Romans; for those Greeks held it to be virtue in a man to lend his wife to a neighbour, and the neighbour to be honored in the loan; yet we Romans would account such doings to be licentious and profligate. But with us, even, it would be more convenient for some if the order of the vices and virtues were changed. For my own part, as matters are, I have but a faint hope of salvation; yet, if the worship of woman and the love of wine were but two of the cardinal virtues, I might hope to be the most illustrious saint in the calendar.

CRIS. But 'tis the bent of man to sin, friend; and were the fashion, as thon call'st it, changed, we should then practice the old-fashioned virtues in our desire to be fashionable in vice. What then, friend?

BEN. Then, my lord, you have only to change back the fashion, and you have the true Christian virtues desired.

CRIS.—Ha, ha, ha! I thank thee for thy counsel, but cannot see therefrom how we may amend the laws. This virtue is a light to guide, not a garment to be worn, that changes shape with the whims and oddities of men and times.

BAS. This fellow is either a presumptuous boor or the veriest fool it has been my lot to look upon.

BEN. If you look as often in your glass as from your toilet I believe, so often you see a greater fool than I.

    BAS. (*striking him*). Audacious slave, let this thy
        manners mend.

BEN. A soldier, and a blow! By heaven and hell, I will not take it from thee. (*Strikes back.*)

    BAS. (*drawing*). Thy life, presumptuous dog, shall
        pay that blow.

CRISPUS *rushes between them, and seizes* BASILIUS *by the wrist.*

CRIS. Pray, good Basilius, moderate your ire.
A soldier may not meekly brook a blow.
You did provoke him first.

    BAS. *(struggling).*   I'll have his life.

    CRIS. Benevolentius, on thy life, withdraw.
I do command thee hence.

    BEN.   I go, my lord.   [*Exit.*

    BAS. My lord, unhand me, or my rage may turn
E'en on yourself.

    CRIS.   How, braggart! Thus I cast,
As spray from rock, thy rage from my disdain.

CRISPUS *throws* BASILIUS *down, and, flinging his sword from him, walks up the stage.*

    BAS. O, well, my lord, it doth become a prince,
Whose state is his impunity, to put
Upon a noble this indignity.

    CRIS. I am a prince, Basilius, but I am
A soldier and a man. If thou art wronged,
And couldst in fair and manly combat find
Thy satisfaction, when and where thou wilt,
I shall be ready.

    BAS.   You shall hear, my lord,
Of this again.

    SEMP. *(aside to Basilius).* If thou wouldst have revenge,
Leave brawling fights to fools, and work below.
Withdraw with me, and I'll unfold a plan
Whereby the pillar of his state and fame,
Already shaken in his father's love,
Thou mayst make reel and fall.

    BAS.   Show me but means,
By violence or craft—I care not how—
To drain the hot blood from his haughty veins,

And make his liver white he thinks mine,
And puling pity shall not balk revenge.

CRIS. A truce, Basilius. Let us look upon
This brawl as rather accident than spleen.
The pride of all was wounded, yet to none
Has serious evil happened. Take my hand,
Which in the name of peace I tender thee.

BAS. Not I, my lord. A rock by lightning cleft
From peak to base, outsplitting two from one,
May take its joint solidity again
Sooner than we be friends.

CRIS.   Nay, then, away!
If thou lov'st better enmity than peace,
Thy rancour shall grow fat on my contempt.

SEMP. (aside). Come, come, Basilius—come away
        with me. [Exeunt SEMPRONIUS and BASILIUS.

MAN. You there have made an enemy, my lord,
'Twere well to watch. I know Basilius well.
An insult, real or fancied, never fades
From his malignant memory ; and the tide
May not more certainly be cast to flow
Than his attempts at vengeance to be made.

CRIS. I do not fear him, Mannius. Name him not.

Re-enter BENEVOLENTIUS.

BEN. I am told, my lord, but will not vouch as true,
that Manlius has revolted.

CRIS. What say'st thou, sirrah ? Manlius revolted ?

BEN. So it is rumoured about the court, my lord; but
'tis told under breath, as though the knowledge had been
gained by eavesdropping rather than published.

CRIS. Now, on my life, I hope the rumour 's true,
For I am weary of inaction here,
And 'tis an honourable task to bring
A traitor to his doom. Disperse you now.
I must resolve the truth of this report,

And, if I find it true, prepare for Gaul.   [*Exeunt.*

SCENE 3.—Another Part of the Palace.

Enter CONSTANTINE *and* SEMPRONIUS.

CON. I hear that Crispus hath to-night held rout,
That thou wast there, and that the whole discourse
Went treasonward.

SEMP. (*aside*).   So, then, my messenger
Has well fulfilled his errand.

CON.   Let me hear
From thine own lips, whose trustiness I know,
The pith and purport of this villainy.

SEMP. There was, my liege, some speech about a
          dream
That Crispus had, which, being told, called forth
Much speculation and opinion—talk
I would I had not lived to listen to.
But then, my lord, 'twas in the heat of wine.

CON. 'Twas in his guilty heart, man, and the wine
Came, like a torch, its perfidy to show.

SEMP. Though I may fear— In mercy, sire, forbear
To question me.   The love I bear your son—
'Twould break my heart to speak aught ill of him ;
And since, alas, I cannot here speak well,
Let love excuse me.

CON.   Nay, perforce I'll know.

SEMP. No force shall move me to the Cæsar's harm.
My love were not o'ertaxed to die for him.

CON. If thou lov'st me, Sempronius, by thy love
I do conjure thee, speak.

SEMP.   I love you both ;
And when my duty sways my love to you,
Then pity comes and sways it back to him.
I would I could be just and not severe.
Although—your pardon—I refuse to speak,

If 'twere your highness' pleasure to give ear
To young Basilius, he heard all, my liege.
He is an honest gentleman, and though
Your son affronted him, still, in the telling,
His honour o'er his anger will be ward,
And will the truth sift from his enmity.
Shall he be called, my lord?

  Con.   Go, bring him hither.

            [*Exit* Sempronius.

He hangs about me like a filthy cloud,
And in a black mist smothers up my peace.
He present, what am I? A withered old,
Wherefrom the glance of ceremony glides
In formal deference as soon as seen ;
And he's the mark and object of the hour,
To which all eyes incline. He'd have me swerve
And turn aside my dim and faded age
To give a place for his enkindling years.
He would—as the Egyptian boors of yore
Did with their fathers' mummies—lay me by,
And on my arid carcase borrow loan,
But know, aspiring younker, that the hand
Which gave the plumage that hath made thee proud
Can yet unfledge and pluck thee. Let me see.

           [*Retires up stage.*

  Re-enter Sempronius, *with* Basilius.

 Semp. Now feed his jealousy, but do't with skill.
Do not, with bungling malice, gorge him full,
Or he may puke, and cast thy slander up ;
But give't with cunning, as reluctantly,
That his keen relish crave and gape for more
(As gapes the sop-fed infant for the spoon)
Ere thou show'st haste to give. This is the way
To make thy grudge of spite against the son
(Being well digested—mixing with the blood)

Flow in the father's veins.

BAS. Fear not my care.

[SEMPRONIUS *moves towards wing.* •

CON. Go not away, Sempronius. I doubt not
Our friend's integrity; but stay thou here,
That if his wounded pride or anger tempt
His judgment into error, and construe
Or strain too strongly aught against my son,
Thy love may interpose to temper it.

SEMP. I stay, my liege. You could not on me lay
A duty more delightful to my love.

BAS. What may, my liege, your pleasure be with me?

CON. Thy memory cannot backward go, Basilius,
Upon the trail of time to any hour
When thou didst know me not?

BAS. O, no, my lord.
Your face seems blended with my reason's dawn,
And of your grace I no beginning know,
More than I know when first I saw the light.

CON. Thy father grew with me, and with me fought,
Advanced in honour with me as in age,
And ever, though declining from my state,
Rose level with my heart; and aye his thrift
Hath in my favour borne abundant fruit.

BAS. This, too, my lord, I also know full well.

CON. Then, therefore shouldst thou love and honour
    me.

BAS. And heaven I take to witness that I do,
Most loyally and reverentially.

CON. Is not defence an attribute of love?

BAS. It is, my liege.

CON. And should, like armour, come
Betwixt love's object and the edge of ill?

BAS. It should, indeed.

CON. And 'tis hypocrisy

Which, knowing danger, still professeth love,
Yet warneth not ?

Bas.   My lord, 'ts treachery.
It is more safe to meet an open foe
Than trust as friend an enemy concealed.

Con. Now on thy logic will I tax thy love.
I have of late had reason to suspect
That treason lurks about my court, and plots
Against my life and power.   I have to-day
An edict drawn, which shall be published straight,
Wherein, inviting evidence from all,
I promise with my proper eye to look
Into the truth, and with my proper ear
To listen to all plaints ; and furthermore,
To give indemnity to loyal men
Whose love may drive suspicion to offence,
Though it should touch the nearest of our kin.

Bas. I trust, my liege, that you deceive yourself.

Con. Be not so coy, Basilius, for I know
That thou to-night hast revelled with my son,
And that from him and others thou didst hear
Discourse unseemly for a son to speak
Or friend to listen to.   Come, is't not so ?

Bas. In truth, my lord, I cannot well deny
That I heard much which jarred upon my love,
And something on my loyalty, to you.

Con. Ah, ah!   Indeed!

Bas.   And for resenting it,
The Cæsar so did sting me with disdain
(Not sparing e'en the insult of his hands)
That, if his proud blood had not been your own,
I could have found the heart to let it forth,
E'en with my sword.   Therefore, my gracious liege,
I will not trust my tongue to speak of him.

Con. I do, by all the love thou dost profess

For me, adjure thee, lay me bare the truth.
Thou say'st he is thy foe.   I am thy friend;
And this, thy foe, is foe no less to me;—
Thou know'st it well—I read it in thy face.
If, in thy manly scorn, thou canst not stoop
To cry complaint of thine own grievances,
Yet, if thou fail'st to warn me from the ill
Whereof I stand in danger from his hate,
Such sulky reticence becomes a crime,
And makes thee guilty as the foe thou shield'st,
'Gainst me, thy menaced friend.

BAS.   Thus pressed, my lord,
I may not longer hesitate to speak.
In brief, I gathered this from what I heard:
That in the order and content that reigns—
The fair fruit of your wisdom—o'er the realm,
The Cæsar sees the grub that marks decay,
And looks with wistful and regretful eye
Aback upon the healthy olden days
When men's free voices called good men to rule
And foster freedom.   Thus, sire, spoke your son;
Yet Mannius was more forward, e'en than he.

CON. Ah, Mannius!   I have known him for a knave
These many years.   We'll deal with him anon.

BAS. Your son the Cæsar had to-night a dream—
At least, my lord, he said it was a dream—

CON. Ay, ay, a dream—with open eyes—a dream!

BAS. And in this dream two men of ancient Rome
Appeared to him, whom he with warmth described,
Commenting on that Liberty, now dead,
Whose shade, he said, they were, which words, my lord,
I grieve to say, were cheered most boisterously.

CON. Ay, he did angle for't—ay, angled well.
Well, well, Basilius, was this all his dream?

BAS. O, no, my liege.   When these did melt away,

There came a second vision, of yourself,
Decked as absurdly as in life you are.
So said he.

SEMP.   No; he said not so, Basilius.

CON. God bless thee for denying this, Sempronius.
He could not say't.

BAS.   Alas, my lord, he did.
I would not, sire, unpressed, have said a word,
But, having spoken—heard my truth impugned—
I challenge, on his probity and honour,
Sempronius to deny it.

CON.   What say'st thou?

SEMP. Was ever kindly heart so sorely tried?
I brand as false, most falsely, a true friend
If I deny; if truly I confirm,
I injure one—though perhaps less true—more dear.

CON. O, father ne'er was cursed with such a child!
O, hypocrite! O, hypocrite!

SEMP. (aside to Basilius). Strike home.

BAS. You were so painted and bedecked with hues
And gems, that he described you as a doll,
And said your gracious person, like your power,
Needs all the paint and gilding of your pomp
To hide its rottenness.

CON.   Thou tell'st a lie!
Does he not lie, Sempronius?

SEMP.   Would he did!

BAS. I fear, indeed, my liege, I anger you.
Pray let me say no more.

CON.   Nay, nay—go on.
'Tis what thou dost not say that frights my most,
For well I know thou glozest what thou say'st.

BAS. Two wretched bondsmen at your feet did kneel,
Whose tongues with servile baseness (this he said
As if impelled to vomit) licked your shoes.

This vision, in commenting, he declared
To be the symbol of the Roman world
Under your gracious and benignant rule.
"And yet"—to pity changing from disgust,
Half smiling, too, as with a kindly scorn—
"And, yet," he said, "my father is grown old."
And then he whispered—what, I did not hear,
But something 'twas that made all laugh that heard,
Ay, and laugh loudly; he laughed loudly too.
Then, waxing grave (the mirth contemptuous o'er),
He said, "Now, when I am"—and here again
He whispered something, ending,—"things will change,
And buried Freedom burst her gilded grave."
On this there rose a shriek of wild applause;
Some hailed him as their future Emperor,
And several cried, "God speed the happy day!"

CON. O, never shall they live to see him throned,
Nor he to wear this diadem of mine.
He hath offended thee?

BAS.   So grievously,
That, but I fear thereby to anger you—

CON. Come thou aside, Basilius   Anger me?
O, no.   Sempronius will forestall thee, and—
Sempronius, retire; I would confer
In private with Basilius.

SEMP.   I obey.
God guide your counsels to a just resolve.   [Exit.

CON. I understand thee; thou wouldst fight my son.
Well, if my son hath wronged thee, 'tis thy due
He give thee satisfaction.   Canst prevail?
Thou art, I know, most skilful with the sword;
But so is Crispus.

BAS.   Good my liege, I fear
Nor sword nor skill, if you be not offended.

CON. Not I offended.   Shouldst thou even kill him—

Thou understandest, shouldst thou even kill him—
In the correction of a righteous cause,
Which sure thou hast— Why, even in thy love
He hath opposed and thwarted thee.
   BAS.   My lord,
Touch not that open sore.
   CON.   But is't not true,
That thou didst woo, with some fair hope to win,
Helena to thy love ?
   BAS,   Too true, my lord,
And that he therein crossed me is too true.
   CON. Why, then, chastise him, man. Upon my life,
I almost hate him for these wrongs of thine.
On any harm he purposeth to me
I can afford to smile, for hopeless 'tis —
If such a thing were possible to be—
As if, of some tall venerable tree,
A branch or bough should in rebellion turn
Upon the root that feeds and nurtures it;
But for his injuries and slights to thee
I could discharge my wrath upon his head.
Fear not to anger me. But—dost thou hear ?—
Make sure of thine own safety. Shouldst thou fall,
His were the triumph, thine the chastisement.
Make sure, Basilius. It must be in fight ;—
What busy tongues call murder must not be,
For thereupon the searching eye of law
And social order dares not drop the lid.
It must be done in fight, and it should seem
As fair and honest. But make sure thyself—
Make sure of thine own safety, as thou mayst.
                Enter CRISPUS.
   CRIS. My lord and father, I have heard the news,
That Manlius has dared revolt in Gaul,
And with impatience I await your word

To bear upon my sword your just rebuke
Against the traitor's heart.

Con.   Thou art too hot.
This zealous heat, methinks, needs time to cool;
And I have views and uses for thee here.

Cris. But first, my liege, I would set right this wrong.
My indiscretion, that did trust the knave,
Doth almost make me guilty of the ill;
And, good my lord, my honour holds me bound
In person to rebuke him.

Con.   'Tis to me
The injury is done, and 'tis for me
To hurl the lance of justice on the slave.
Content thee where thou art, for 'tis my will
To send, upon this errand of revenge,
Constantius into Gaul.

Cris.   You do me wrong.

Con. 'Tis thy presumption, boy, that speaks of wrong.
I'd have thee know thy place. Content thee here,
For I for thee have other use and views,
And I have said, Constantius goes to Gaul.   [*Exit,*

Bas. (*aside*). This is my first instalment of revenge.
                                 [*Exit.*

Cris. How have I earned this slight? I know not how,
For I have ever with the firmest faith
Repaid the trust he lent. Methinks there seems
A lukewarmness and reticence of late,
About my father's commerce with myself,
That savours of distrust; and yet so slow,
So gradual hath been the growth—and I
(Unapprehensive and unwarned of ill)
Have noted it so negligently, too—
That in the suddenness of my disgrace
I read my peril backward, and discern
Too late the dangers of false confidence.

So one may stand upon a treacherous beach,
Forecasting no mischance, and see the tide
Steal in and round on the inconstant sands,
Yet wake not unto danger till the sea's
Insidious rising cuts him off from shore.
Such is my fortune.   What is to be done?
Am I the dupe of evil envious tongues,
Or is it but the humour of my sire ?
There's more in it than this.   The more I think,
More of design I see, and less of chance.
By heaven, I'm watched!   I'm played upon by spies!
Now I remember earnest eyes and ears,
Much whispering, some peeping, creaking shoes,
Which oft betray the listener ; and of late
I scarce can ever find myself alone.
If that my father—whose confiding faith
Should buoy my spotless honour, as the main
Doth float my stately galley—doubts my truth,
And lets me from his favour fall like lead
Into the ooze and muddle of mistrust,
Setting about me rascals to betray,
I know my worth and dignity too well
To bend me to such treatment, though to bend
Might yet forefend my breakage.   If it be,
Again, some passing humour, some strange whim,
Whereto infirmity and age are prone,
And which some later oddity may mend,
My patience must endure it.   Till I prove,
I'll try to bear, for, if he use me ill,
He is my sovereign and my father still.   [*Exit.*

ACT III.

SCENE 1.—The Grounds about the Palace.

HELENA *and* SERVIA.

HEL. Some other time.   I will not hear it now.

SER. O lady, lady, let me tell you now;
For it imports your happiness to know,
And on my mind it lies a heavy load.

HEL. Thou superstitious girl, wilt have no nay?
Well, well, be brief, or Crispus will be here.

SER. When, lady, early yesternight I stole,
Oppressed with heat and headache, from the court
To seek the cool refreshment of the air,
Soon as mine eyes, galled by the palace glare,
Befit the gloom (the moon being under cloud),
A sight most strange did greet them.   'Twas as though
The jewelled firmament had dropped its gems,
And all the stars, with moving life endued,
Flit here and there among the shrubs and flowers.

HEL. Why, 'tis the fire-fly, Servia, thou hast seen.

SER. Perchance it may have been, sweet lady, though
In such strange multitude and beauteous fire
As ne'er I saw before.   Anon they fled,
Till dwindling distance veiled them from the eye,
Save one, which almost at my feet remained.
I slowly sunk unto the ground, and lay
With eye almost upon it.   In my gaze,
Whose keenness dwarfed myself, it seemed to grow,
And, on a bud that with the weak wind waved,
Like maid at mirror, sat a fairy form,
Her tresses braiding by a bead of dew.
I, from the movement of her lips, perceived
That she did speak or sing, and bent mine ear
With such acuteness that all nature seemed

To shrink into the compass of mine eye ;
And then in plaintive melody I heard
This song, that lies so heavy at my heart.

SONG.

Now in the moonlight may happy maids sleep,
  Love in their bosoms, like pearl in bright shells;
While the forlorn ones lie watching, and weep,
  Tears in their eyelids, like dewbeads in bells.

Yet may the Princess Helena rest well,
  Peace in her breast, still unused to deceit,
On whose fair lips and cheeks rare beauties dwell,
  Where they like roses lie, lovely and sweet.

Soon o'er her young life a cloud shall impend,
  Gloomy November shall shadow her May
Care, like a vulture, her quiet shall rend,
  Into her beauty creep grub-like decay.

For, in an ambush that lies by her way,
  Sly as the adder, a rival doth glide,
Who in her envy the loved one shall slay,
  Leaving the lorn one to waste by his side.

HEL. In sooth, I wish thou hadst not told me this.

SER. The singing ended, I did clutch the flower,
When, as if waking from a horrid trance,
All vanished, and, affrighted, damp, and chill,
I fled into the house and sought my bed.

HEL. Why, thou hast dreamt. I'm glad 'tis but a
    dream,
For hope lay in me like a trampled flower.

SER. Alas, 'twas not a dream. Behold the bud !

HEL. Give me the bud, thou silly child. No word
Of this to Crispus, for his own grave cares
Need not the weight of these thy childish fears.

Enter CRISPUS.

SER. Farewell, sweet Princess. Heaven defend you
    both.   [*Exit.*

CRIS. I greet thee, dear one, now my only joy !
Why did thy maid, on leaving, look so sad ?

Keep those about thee that have fairer skins.
Have all things light around thee, love.   And yet,
Her swarthy face, though sorrowful, looks kind.

HEL. O, yes.   She loves me, and her tawny skin
And homely features, in the light of love
(For 'tis the light that makes all nature fair),
Look beautiful to me.

CRIS.   The light is all.
There is not in the world a face so plain,
A form so shapeless or uncouthly knit,
Which, being lit by kindly soul within,
Does not look beautiful—more lovely, far,
Than all the carved perfections of the face,
Than all the sculptured graces of the form,
Unwarmed and unillumined by goodwill.
The coarse and homely lantern whose light cheers
And guides the homebound wanderer o'er the wild
Is far more grateful to the traveller's need
Than the most costly lamp that gold and gems
And skill could fashion, wanting oil and flame.
See what the light of heaven alone can do,
How gild the misty unsubstantial clouds!
The west is all aflame with auric fire.
Didst ever see sun set so gorgeously?
Lo, yonder sheet of pale pellucid blue,
Which seems a calm lake, girt by golden shores,
Wherein the aching eye, as 'twere, may bathe,
And find refreshment from the heavenly glare.
Why, e'en the dusky east, where stealthy shades
Of coming night creep up into the sky,
Hath here and there a touch of tender rose.

HEL. Alas, 'tis evanescent as our joy!
If here we linger but a little while,
We may observe it fade e'en while we watch.

CRIS. It lies not in the potency of art,

Were all tho priceless treasures of the world,
In gold and silver, gems, and precious pearls,
By kings and fairies yielded for the trial,
So to assort and blend them as to show
A spectacle so gorgeous as yon clouds.
Yet all is naught but vapours and the sun,
And those same vapours would, without the sun,
Look dark and threatening.   So, the light is all.

HEL. O, Crispus, Crispus, much too like, alas!
Are thine own fortunes to those faithless clouds,
For in the radiance of thy father's love
Thy future all as dazzling looked as they;
But now, alas, that his good favour wanes
And ebbs away, thy golden hopes wax grim,
And frown as darkly as those vapours will
When they have lost the lustre of the sun.

CRIS. Fret not for me, Helena, for my grief,
Heavy though 'tis, hath counterpoising joy.
If I'm withheld from honourable war,
I am devised to thee.   Whilst of my fame
The laurel droops, my bud of love shall blow;
And as the oyster, of the sandy grit
That in his homely shell intrudes to gall,
Doth make a precious pearl, so, sweet, will I,
Of this my trouble, make my heart more rich
In treasure of thy dear devoted love.

HEL. Could my devotion such dear wealth bestow
As thy love has endowed my breast withal,
Then should thy heart be all encased in pearl.
But soft, we are observed, for this way wing
The courtly butterflies.   Regard them not.

*Several Ladies and Courtiers cross the stage giggling, who nod
negligently to* CRISPUS *and* HELENA.

CRIS. Pass on, ye light and flimsy moths of men.
Too well I see ye know of my disgrace.

Like feathers i' the air, your courtly leers
Show which way sits the wind.

    More Courtiers pass by, as before.   •

            Ay, amble on.

  HEL. O, Crispus, heed them not.

  CRIS.   See, scarce to-day
They to my broken fortunes deign to nod
Who to my honours would have kissed the ground.

  HEL. They will but anger thee. O, let's away.

    Others pass in the same way.

  CRIS. Away, ye gilded vermin—get ye gone.
These insects, Helen, that now show their stings,
To-morrow, if my father smiled on me,
Would bring me all the honey from their hives.
Such men are friends but as our shadows are,
Appearing only when the sun doth shine.
Had Jove like mice or beetles fashioned them,
Their bodies were too noble for their souls.

    Enter SEMPRONIUS *and* BASILIUS.

  SEMP. (*aside*). Hast thou, as I advised thee, tipped
      thy sword
With subtle poison?

  BAS.   Ay, and the whole blade
Reeks with the keener venom of my hate.

  SEMP. 'Tis well. (*Saluting Crispus respectfully*):

        My lord, I know your heavy shame,
And could not, if my own, more deeply grieve.
A film has gathered on your father's eye
That clouds your honest worth; yet not for long.
Time and his love will purge it, never fear.
In sooth, I hope it will.

  CRIS.   I thank thee, friend.

  SEMP. I will not stay, my lord. No witness by,
Basilius, doubtless, like a noble soul,
Will court the peace that he so lately spurned.

Cris. Then comes his friendship welcome as a staff
To crippled limbs.   [*Exit* Sempronius.
(Basilius *stares at* Crispus, *and smiles maliciously.*)
                    What may this mean, Basilius?
Why with this rudeness dost thou look on me?
  Bas. A cat, 'tis said, may look upon a king.
Then why may not patrician eyes look down
Upon a fallen Cæsar?
  Cris.   Helen, go.
  Hel. O, heaven defend us! I will seek for help. [*Exit.*
  Cris. Beware, Basilius! I am almost wild.
I would not have thy death upon my soul.
Hast aught to say?
  Bas.   I have.
  Cris.   Then say't at once,
And quickly, and away. What wouldst thou say?
  Bas. That I rejoice that some miraculous power
Should, seeing that thou mayst not go to Gaul,
So aptly thus have brought home *gall* to thee.
  Cris. Hence, leering fiend! Why dost thou linger here?
  Bas. To claim the satisfaction of thy life,
Which to my wounded honour long is due. (*Draws.*)
  Cris. (*drawing*). Then take it if thou canst, malignant
        cur.
Crispus *dashes furiously upon* Basilius *and disarms him;*
    then, throwing down his own sword, seizes him by the
    shoulders, but in doing so slips and falls, with Basilius
    upon him. The latter sets himself firmly on Crispus, *one*
    hand to his throat, and draws a dagger.
  Bas. Now, if I quit thee till thy life is mine,
May hell burn off this arm.
Crispus, *with a desperate effort, throws off* Basilius *and*
        rises, taking up the latter's sword.
  Cris. Rise, miscreant, and take again thy sword.
Though thou wouldst murder, I was born for war.

Basilius rises and takes up the other sword.

BAS. (*aside*). Confusion! he has got the poisoned sword.
My lord, I claim that weapon. This is yours.

CRIS. Thou hast a weapon. Quick! upon thy guard,
Assassin, ere I strike thee down unarmed.

The fight, and BASILIUS *falls.*

O, wretched hour! What fruit doth fury bear!

Re-enter HELENA, *with* SEMPRONIUS, FAUSTA, *Servants, &c.*

SEMP. My lord, my lord, you have not killed my friend?
Alas, too sadly true!

HEL.   O, luckless youth!
I could not love thee, yet I pity thee.

FAUSTA. O, Crispus, Crispus, why didst thou do this?
This ghastly vision shakes my soul with grief,
And of mine eyes makes hands to wring my heart.

CRIS. Your sorrow, lady, is but as a shadow
Unto the bulk and substance of my grief.

SEMP. Bear off the body. Fly, my lord, at once.
Basilius was in favour high at court,
And I do fear the anger thy sire.   [*Body borne off.*

CRIS. Why should I fly, Sempronius? Cowards fly.
I am a soldier and a soldier's son,
And, for my father's honour and my own,
I'll answer like a soldier for this deed.

SEMP. At least, my lord, withdraw into the court.
If you disdain to shirk your father's ire,
It is not meet that you should linger here.
See, all around you curious eyes abound,
And busy blabbing tongues, and thoughtless brains.
It will but add vexation to your grief
To be the mark and witness of such things.
In order's name, let me beseech you, sir,
At once, with the fair Princess, to withdraw.

CRIS. Thy counsel's given with a friendly will;
It is, moreover, wise; and I obey

With friendly readiness.   Come, then, my joy !
Be thou my comforter.   Though troubles grow,
Though honours fade, and friendships fall away,
I've wealth in thee.   As other lights die out,
Thou brighter grow'st, my solitary star.

[*Exeunt* CRISPUS *and* HELENA.

FAUSTA. Ere long a cloud shall settle on that star.
We may, Sempronius, from this deadly brawl,
Contrive a means to tear this pair atwain,
And as a lever use Helena's love
To overturn her lover's confidence.
I will at once alarm Helena's fears,
Exaggerate the wrath of Constantine,
Profess belief his fury will arraign
The Cæsar for the murder of Basilius.
She knows how ill in odour stands the son
Already in the nostrils of the sire,
And hence will quail in terror for his life
If in the Emperor's present humour tried.
But I will tell her that delay would sooth
My husband's anger, and so Crispus save.
I will be lavish of my condolence,
And, whilst my own inaction I excuse,
Lest I by meddling should my lord offend,
I'll show her how a little guiltless guile
May gain delay, and ask her dare she risk't.

SEMP. She'll tell you she would hazard life and soul
On such a venture.

FAUSTA.   This, then, is my plan:
I'll tell the Princess that a spurious writ,
For the arrest and exile of the Cæsar,
Shall in her hands be placed, which she must give
To one that bringeth her a secret word.
That Crispus shall be then conveyed to Rome,
And there detained until my husband's ire

Shall have a time to cool, and where herself
Shall presently rejoin him and explain.
There, I will tell her—as, indeed, she knows—
The Emperor and his court will shortly be
To celebrate his twenty years of reign,
'Mid the rejoicings of which festival
The father's ire shall soften towards the son,
And all again be peace. But, mark you me:
I will, meantime, a genuine writ procure,
And not a counterfeit, which, under seal,
Shall be for use confided to her care.
You must contrive that some one of the guard
May come upon her with that secret word
In presence of the Cæsar. Dost thou see?

SEMP. I see your highness' drift, but likewise see
Some risk that her bewilderment may cause
An explanation, and defeat your scheme.

FAUSTA. But little risk. It must, at least, be run,
For naught that's human can be surely gaged.
She'll give the paper; and 'tis likely, too,
That she, in her amazement, will retire
To 'scape ill-timed discovery. If so,
I will be ready to receive her there,
And, till she's safely on the road to Rome,
She shall not quit my sight. When Crispus finds
Himself a prisoner, and the Princess flown,
Can he then doubt of her perfidiousness?

SEMP. But what of Crispus?

FAUSTA.   That of him that may.

SEMP. But when they meet all this will be explained,
And your deceit exposed.

FAUSTA.   They shall not meet.
I will consign her into trusty care.
The simple wench will, if she lives, grow crazed,
Unless she proveth tougher than she seems;

But, if her senses keep perversely sane,
And I should, haply, find that danger grows,
Her death shall be my safety. Fare you well.
I must at once in motion put my scheme.   [*Exit.*

SEMP. That she loves Crispus I am all but sure,
And that I therefore hate him, sure indeed ;
But to believe that Crispus could love her,
To the infringement of his father's honour,
I know his high and noble soul too well.
Then, knowing this, I such honour prize ;
Yet, that he dazzles where I fain would shine
Sufficeth for my hate. I'll bide my time ;
I'll watch my lady's plotting for a while ;
Once certain that her plottings that way tend,
I'll cross them with some plottings of my own.   [*Exit.*

SCENE 2.—Neighbourhood of the Palace.
Enter PAPPUS.

PAP. Why should men wish to live to be old, when every
new day brings with it new vexations ? Crispus has killed
Basilius, and thereby put his own life in jeopardy. What
was Basilius, that the Cæsar should stand in danger for
killing him ? An impudent saucy coxcomb that had no
reverence for age. I am older than his grandfather, had
he lived, would be now, and I have never had a courteous
word from his uncivil tongue. But Crispus—may heaven
requite him for it!—honoureth grey hairs. 'Tis not long
ago that, walking abroad, I encountered the two, and let
fall my staff in saluting them, the recovery whereof my
lumbago rendered very difficult. Observing my trouble,
Basilius—ungracious coxcomb—stood laughing at me ; but
the Cæsar, bending his royal back to raise it, restored it
to me with the sweetest of smiles and the kindest of
words. Danger forsooth ! The Cæsar should be praised
by old men for killing every such jackanapes ; and Con-

stantine is getting old.   The old fool—there's nobody by—
yes, the old fool, for he is an old fool—not content with
taking away his son's command, must be angry with him
because he kills the puppy Basilius.   I have no patience—
an old goose.   He is blind—the Emperor is blind—blind
as justice.   Nay, would he were so blind ; but he is only
blind in one eye and jaundiced in the other.   He turns
the dark eye to his son's virtues, and colours his faults
with the diseased one.

Enter BENEVOLENTIUS.

BEN. Well met, Pappus.   I have news that will do thy
heart good.

PAP. What is it, princox?   Is the Emperor dead?

BEN. The gods forbid, Pappus, for that would grieve
thee ; but Basilius is, and the Cæsar like to be.   And I
know thou wilt agree with me, that the world will be well
rid of him.

PAP. Thou art a fool.

BEN. Not so, Pappus.   I was once a fool, but, thanks to
thy teaching, I have since grown wise.

PAP. To my teaching ?   Then I am ashamed of my
scholar.

BEN. Ay, to thy teaching, Pappus.   I did think Crispus
wise, well-looking, and possessed of every quality that
makes men amiable and princes worshipful ; but I have
noted him narrowly of late, and find him a very dunce, a
blockhead, a—

PAP. Thou art a dunce and a blockhead to call him so.

BEN. I have looked at him through thy spectacles, and
where I erewhile saw beauties I now only see blemishes.
I have seen his legs, too; and thou wast right, Pappus,—
he is both bandy and back-shinned.

PAP. Shame on thy ribald tongue!   Thou art no more
worthy to live in the same age with him than his father
to be his progenitor.

BEN. Nay, Pappus, cry not shame on me, but on thyself, for thou hast been my schoolmaster.

PAP. Can the gods hearken to him and not smite him?

BEN. Ay can they, for the gods know that what I say ill of the Cæsar thou hast taught me; and thou knowest best how wisely.

PAP. Thou didst never hear me speak ill of the Cæsar, whom I love better than my old life—never one ill word. Heaven be my judge, my old heart hath no feeling for him but reverence. And to say I taught thee— Shame on thee, ruffian. And he in trouble, too—(*wipes eyes*)—and he in tribulation.

BEN. Come, come, Pappus, I do but jest. I am sorry to have pressed it so far; but do not weep, old man, albeit thy tears do honour thee.

PAP. Weep, coxcomb? I weep not—'tis a mote in my eye. Weep, indeed! And for the Cæsar, too! What am I to the Cæsar? Were he pitched into the Bosphorus, he should have no tears from me. Weep, forsooth! I weep not, sirrah. 'Tis a mote—'tis a mote in my eye. ⌈*Exit.*

BEN. Thou art a strange old man, Pappus; but thy heart is tender, if thy head be tough.

SCENE 3.—A Room in the Palace.

CRISPUS *and* HELENA.

CRIS. Why art thou thus so restless?

HEL.   O, my lord,
You know that danger hangeth o'er your life,
And should know how I love you. Knowing this,
And conscious, too, that I your peril know,
This question 's idle.

CRIS.   Yet thou weepest not—

HEL. O, that I could!

CRIS.   As was thy wont before
When danger menaced me. Thine eyes are dry.

I have some while observed thee, and thou seem'st
As if thy nerves and sinews all were strung
In pained expectancy.   Thou art not still
Whilst I could reckon four.   Thy fingers move,
Or, if they rest, there 's motion in thy toes ;
Thy lips, though silent, yet are never still,
But twitch and mumble, and whene'er they part,
I see thy tongue at work upon thy teeth ;
Thou risest oft, as thou wouldst something do,
But, doing naught, as oft sitt'st down again ;
Thy restless eye now wanders towards the door,
Now on the ground is cast, and now to heaven.
Methinks at times that thou wouldst speak to me ;
Then, stopping shortly, o'er thy face there steals
A look of anguish, ending in a sigh.
If there is aught that weighs upon thy heart,
Then who so fit to share that weight as I ?

    HEL. (*aside*). O, cursed promise !—thus to bind my
        tongue,
When it were cheap with death to ransom it !

    CRIS. Thou wring'st thy hands, but dost not answer me.
Ah, why thus silent ?   Thou dost look on me,
And on thy face dost wear a tender smile ;
But through thy tenderness I see thy pain,
As through a veil of lace a negro skin.
And though thou ling'rest with me, yet I know
That thou my presence wouldst more gladly shun.

    HEL. O, Crispus, thou wilt tear my heart to rags.
To know thee safe, and die before thee here,
Were bliss celestial ;—parted, life were pain.

    CRIS. There is some secret gnawing at thy peace.

           Enter OFFICER *of the* GUARD.

    OFF. I greet your highnesses with duteous love.
(*Aside*): "Advenio."

    HEL.   Advenio !   That is the hateful word.

O, fearful man, why com'st thou here ? Begone.

OFF. I go, your highness. Will you—

HEL. Do not go.

It must be done, and danger 's in delay.

Take thou this paper. Ask me not a word,

Or strength will fail me ere I get me hence.

O, God! Farewell—my life—my love—farewell. [*Exit.*

CRIS. What is the meaning of this pantomime ?

OFF. I would this fell to other hands than mine.

[*Goes to door and beckons.*

Enter Four Soldiers.

You know, my lord, a soldier's duty leads

Full often where his heart is loth to go.

Such is my case at present. I have here

The warrant of his majesty your father

To apprehend you for a murder, done

On young Basilius.

CRIS. Murder, villain ! No.

I must be calm, for I need all my wits

To comprehend and fathom what I fear.

My fears confirmed, let death or madness come,

For life and reason then were hateful plagues.

Good captain, tell me, and I'll bless thy tongue—

No dawn shall smile, no twilight fade in gloom,

That shall not hear my prayers for thee on high—

O, tell me that the warrant thou dost bear

Thou hadst not from the Princess. Thou dost nod ;

Thou meanest yes—that my good hope is true—

She did not give it. Did she ? O, say no ;

Say no, and swear it—on thy oath say no—

Or be thy life's best pleasures throes and groans,

And never-ending tortures tear thy soul.

Say no—I do beseech thee—O, say no.

OFF. Alas, my lord, the Princess gave it me.

CRIS. False, false! O, God! O, hell-pitched agony!

Off. And here, my lord, by her own hand inscribed,
" See the instructions strictly be obeyed."

Cris. O, had my cup of fortune been distilled
From all that 's sweet in life, this drop of gall
Had made all nauseous.   But her seeming truth
Has been the sweet but solitary drop
That made my draught of being bearable;
That soured and curded in my luckless horn,
Life is not worth the drinking.   Farewell joy!
'Mid all my trials, resting on her faith,
As on a rock 'mid raging waves, I stood
Secure and hopeful.   Crumbling now to sand,
The treacherous footing fails my trusting feet,
And leaves me friendless, hopeless, in the sea.
Yet will I struggle with the surging tide;
My wrongs like bladders buoy me.   I will go
And beard my tyrant father on his throne.

Off. Alas, my lord, I dare not let you pass.
You are a prisoner.

Cris. (drawing).   Prisoner, dog!   Make way,
Or, by my hopeless soul, thy limbs shall feel
The strength of shameful wrongs.

Off.   Good noble sir,
Wreak not your wrath on me, the instrument.
I only do what I dare not refuse.

Cris. Ay, truly; take my sword.   I pawn my word
(And e'en my foes will not impugn the pledge)
To hold myself your prisoner till released
By just authority.   But give me leave,
Upon the surety of a warrior's word,
To go— No; since he leaves me not the power
To go to him—why, let him come to me.
Thou wilt without a Gallic soldier see,
By name Benevolentins; call him here.

Off. I know the man, and met him as I came.   [Exit.

CRIS. Now be my nerve as rigid as my sword.

Re-enter OFFICER, *with* BENEVOLENTIUS.

Thou art an honest trooper and blunt man,
And shufflest not with truth. Wouldst thou, now, fear
To bear a message as 'tis told to thee
Unto the august ear of Constantine ?

BEN. If you gave me a purse of gold to carry to a
friend, my honesty would deliver it as I received it; and
to deliver your message in any words but your own I
should deem false as to substitute base metal for the
pure gold. If I undertake, I will faithfully discharge ;
but ere I engage to carry, I would first know the weight
of the burthen, and an ugly message to Constantine were
no light matter.

CRIS. Tell him that I—the Cæsar he disgraced,
The son he hates, the subject that he wrongs—
My many griefs my titles to command—
Demand an audience of his mightiness ;
And as my fetters, by his order forged,
Let me not hence, 'tis needful he come here.

BEN. I must confess, my lord, that I like not the com-
mission. The offence of the message might be laid to him
that carries it, as the foulness of water may be charged
on a dirty pipe; and an angry monarch is a beast with a
keen bite. But if your highness will only write your
message, I'll take it, though I lose my head for my pains.

CRIS. (*writing*). Thy caution shall defend thy honesty.
Thy ignorance of the contents of this letter
Shall shield thee from all evil consequence.

                    [*Exit* BENEVOLENTIUS *with letter.*

What spirits went my brother in to Gaul ?

OFF. Faith, not the best, my lord, for all the troops
Did cry aloud for you.

CRIS.   I'm sorry for it.
If this rebuff damp not his martial fire,

His worthiness may yet the soldiers win.

Off. Not while you live, my honoured lord, I fear,
Their hearts are so ingrafted on yourself.
Now, were you not the upright prince you are (*whispers*),
From this abundance of the soldiers' love
You might a power arouse to right your wrongs,
And turn the tables on your enemies.

Cris. No more of this, good captain—nay, no more.
On this I wink, as on mistaken love;
Another hint were treason to my sire,
Who only seems my foe. Though he forgets
His princely dignity, I know my own.

Off. My lord, believe me, I'll offend no more.

Cris. Dost thou not shortly follow them to Gaul?

Off. I do, my lord, and presently prepare.

Cris. I'll lay some grateful penance on thy sin.
Thou know'st my brother is a goodly youth,
Of gentle manners, firm of heart, and free,
Of whom experience will a soldier make?

Off. I do, my lord, and love him next to you.

Cris. Spread, then, thy friendly thoughts of him
          abroad
Among the troops, and, serving him, serve me.
Commend him as you deem of his deserts,
But promise nothing he may not perform.
Undue laudation breaks the back of worth.
Betwixt ambition and established fame
There lies a troubled sea. So put him forth,
That, in the fair wind of a modest hope,
The light freight of his merits may achieve
A prosperous voyage. So, you serve him well.
Aid rather with the oars of your goodwill,
Than sink him with the treasure of your praise.

                 Enter Constantine.

Con. Soldiers, retire; but wait within my call.

Lo, thou most high and mighty prince, I'm here ;
The chief of Rome on thy behest attends ;
The father is obedient to the child.
What would your haughty Cæsarship with me ?
    CRIS. Not mercy, which, not having sinned, I spurn,
But justice, which your office should bestow,
Albeit I see your temper will deny it.
And I have wrongs that might have summoned Jove
From his high seat to right them.
    CON.   Guard thy tongue.
If thou hast not had justice done to thee,
It is my mercy that withholdeth it.
    CRIS. 'Tis false—a shameful and a slanderous lie.
    CON. This to thy father, wild unduteous boy ?
    CRIS. Shall I observe the reverence of a son,
While you ignore the duties of a sire ?
    CON. Be heedful what thou say'st, mad, fiery fool ;
For, did not temper in my aging veins
Run low and smoothly, high embanked with patience,
This insolence of thine, like mountain flood,
Had swelled it into rage. But have a care,
Most mighty and indomitable Cæsar ;—
Deep as my channel of endurance lies,
It may be fed till it o'erbears its bounds ;
Then, woe to thee.
    CRIS.   What would you further do ?
All that your power and hate could lay on me
Already have I borne. Except my life—
Which, sooth, you gave me, and are free to take,
As welcomely as if 'twere a disease—
I have no mark to offer to your spleen
Which yet you have not struck. Therefore your threat,
As 'gainst the current of my just complaint,
Is weaker than your breath against the tide.
    CON. What are the grievous wrongs thou mouthest of ?

Cris. What are my wrongs? Ye gods! What are
      my wrongs!
What are the wages of my years of toil?
   Con. Distinction, honours, scarcely less than mine;
And power that now grows threatening to my own.
    Cris. A burning cheek should put your tongue to shame,
For every tribute that my arms could win
Has at your feet been laid.   My borrowed power
Has ever been a butment of your own.
I served you in the west, and in the east,
And served you faithfully where'er I served.
And what hath been the guerdon of my pains?
You grudged the honours that you justly gave,
Plucked off my well-won laurels to plant thorns,
Repaid my wounds with loss of my command,
My truth with doubt, my love with cold disdain,
My conquests with humiliating shame.
   Con. Thou liest, whelp! I grudged thee naught I gave.
While thou couldst bear thee meekly, all was well;
But when thou wouldst, 'gainst him that did bestow,
Uplift the weapon given thee to defend—
Nay, like a cur, wouldst bite the hand that feeds—
And when thou, prating of my reign with scorn,
Wouldst try to sap allegiance to my throne—
I were the veriest fool to trust thee.
   Cris.   Pshaw.
Suspicions are the children of your fear,
Your fear the child of slander.   Fears and doubts
Do on each other breed incestuously,
As quick as vermin.   So they breed in you.
So thickly pestered has your mind become,
That, in its unclean habitation, thought
Is tortured into frenzy; and your spleen,
Rather than chide your own impurity,
Would blame your wholesome neighbour for your plague.

Con. Thou hatchest mischief 'gainst me night and day,
Awake, conspiring to seduce my friends,
And dreaming treason when thine eyes are closed.
O, hypocrite, thou handlest treason well.
When was the world so tranquil as 'tis now ?
Yet, under cover of pretended dreams,
Thou speakest things that make men's hearts disloyal,
Insinuate misprision of my rule,
And plant ambitious hopes in restless minds,
Which, if permitted to take root and grow,
Would set each subject at his neighbour's throat.

   Cris. Be just, old man, for to be just is wise,
And righteous wisdom well beseemeth age.
These are, the calumnies that feed your fears.

   Con. These are no calumnies, but tested truths.
Such things thou dost to creep into my shoes.

   Cris. 'Tis false, and they that tell you so are liars.
You have infested me with pimps and spies
That pander to your malice, and like chains
Have hung their serpent eyes and ears upon me ;
And all they see, or hear, or may surmise,
Distort, discolour, garble, or invent,
Skilled in the relish of a maw diseased,
They dish to suit the palate of your spleen,
And you eat greedily.

   Con.   'Tis false.

   Cris.   'Tis true.

   Con. Abortion ! 'tis a lie.

   Cris.   I say 'tis true.
'Tis thrift to pamper where 'tis loss to cure.
They know the sickling loves to nurse his ills,
And pander to and nourish your disease
In place of physicking.   They mock us both.
You are the dupe, the sacrifice am I ;
And thus it follows, as result from cause,

Where I would trust, I am constrained to fear,
And where I yearn to reverence, to despise.
    Con. Be civil, ingrate—monster that thou art.   •
    Cris. I will be civil when you can be fair.
You wrong me, taunt me, goad me to rebel,
And when you've scorched my patience into flame,
You chide my anger with such fiery rage
That your rebuke outsins the fault it blames.
I pity you, old man, I pity you.
    Con. Devil! I knew thee not. I'll bear no more.
Constantine *strikes at* Crispus *with his sword, but the latter*
    evades the blow, seizing the wrist of his sword arm.
    Cris. See how the vigour of the veteran fails
'Gainst youth and injuries unarmed.
    Con.   Let go.
    Cris. As man, your age is helpless. Play the lord;
Employ your lungs; owe safety to your slaves.
'Tis but to call.
    Con.   Great gods! Wouldst murder?
    Cris.   No,
Not I; nor shall your frenzy murder me
Till I have taught your kingship clemency.
                       [*Wrests the sword from his father.*
But, could a soldier stoop to parricide,
I have you at my mercy, and your throne,
Your purple, sceptre, dignities, and sway,
Upon the point of this same sword, which now
You raised against my life. 'Tis but to thrust,
And all the minions that exalt your pride
(Though they, while yet you have the strength to call,
Would on your bidding tear my entrails out)
Will, if they find you dead, shriek out my praise,
And say I have done well. Then think of this
Until your dying day—that from this hour,
The brief remainder of your life you owe

To my forbearance.

Con.   Give me back my sword,
And arm thyself with whatsoe'er thou wilt,
And, by the gods, I will not live an hour,
If, with the prowess of this arm alone,
I fail to punish thee, thou saucy slave.

Cris. I hold my honour dearer than my life.
If might afflicts, yet virtue can endure ;
If wrong provokes, yet nature can subdue.
You are my father—would you were not so—
And in that name have title to this sword.
There is your weapon ; I am all unarmed,
Save in the armour of my innocence ;
Here 's my defenceless bosom—cleave't atwain ;
Look, look within—survey my springs of life—
And there see honour, honesty, and truth,
And let the thought of how you valued them
In hues of blood suffuse your cheeks with shame.
Nay, do not hesitate.   You wish me dead ;
Strike, and in striking do an act more kind
Than aught you've done to me these many days.

Con. I will not strike ; yet, that I strike thee not,
And send thy churlish insolence to hell,
Is weakness—weakness.   Thou mayst pity me.
                              [*Throws down the sword.*

Cris. Is death too great a mercy at your hands?
What, too great honour for your angry pride
To let my soul escape upon your sword ?
Ay, you reserve me for a shameful end,
Upon a shameless charge.   Well, do your worst.

Con. Didst thou not kill Basilius ?
Cris.   I did ;
And in your cause a hundred better men.

Con. Thou gloriest in the butchery.
Cris.   Not so,

For all I could, I did, his life to spare.
He would have murdered me.

 Con.   Thou liest, knave ; •
But thou didst murder him to screen thyself.
He was my friend, and knew thee for a traitor.

  Cris. A traitor?

  Con.   Ay ; Basilius told me so.

  Cris. Basilius lied.

  Con.   Thou plott'st against my life.

  Cris. Against your life ? The breath that gives you
    power
To speak this odious calumny is due
To mercy, and from me. Against your life!

  Con. Against my life and power.

  Cris.   Ungrateful man.
Shame on your graceless age, that thus repays
A faithful servitor for honest pains.
I have into your diadem put gems,
Eked out your sceptre and enlarged its range,
And your enfolding purple, by the half,
Have made more ample.

  Con.   Guards! Enough of this.

    Enter Officer *and Guards.*
Seize on that blatant and rebellious boy,
And put the boasting braggart into chains.

    Guards seize Crispus.

  Cris. O, sovereign father—emperor—honoured lord—
Command me unto prison, into chains,
And I will go, obedient to your word.
But look—vile hands are on my person laid ;
And think, I am your flesh and blood, your son.

  Con. Take off your brutish clutches from my son.
Let go, or, by my sceptre and my soul,
I'll have you hanged.   [*Guards release* Crispus.

  Off.   Your pardon, good my liege ;

What we have done we did not for ourselves,
But on your mandate.

    Con.   Must we be betrayed
In our authority by nimble slaves
That take our weak caprices for commands,
And have our hasty petulance obeyed
Ere thought has time to right it ?

    Off.   Let me hope,
Most royal master, that the same good thought
Which now revokes the order may condone
The sin of our obedience.

    Con.   Get thee gone,
With thy obedience and forward zeal,
Or I will bid thee cut thy saucy throat,
And see thou dost obey.   Thy warrant, knave.
                                [*Snatches warrant.*
Take your detested faces from my sight.
                        [*Exeunt* Officer *and Soldiers.*

    Cris. The God of Hosts be thanked, my gracious lord!
That flash of anger to your bosom came
Like lightning in the night, revealing there
Paternal fondness still, which doubt obscured.
O, father, take me to your love once more.
I do repent my rashness, and recall
Whate'er my tongue hath uttered of offence,
And to my knees am bowed with self-reproof.
O, tear aside mistrust's estranging veil—
Withdraw the sluice that dams your breast with doubt,
And let me gush into your heart again.

    Con. (*aside.*) O, how this old heart tugs against my
            will,
Like an impatient charger on the rein.
'Twould leap on him, and the relaxing nerve
Of my displeasure scarce can hold it in.
This posture well becomes thy penitence,

And penitence thy sin.   But thou mayst rise.
To stay too long on supplicating knees
Becometh not the son of Constantine.

    CRIS. Vouchsafe to say that I arise forgiven.

    CON. Too soon, too soon, my son.   Thy fault is green,
And thy contrition needs the test of time.
It is a trick of many evil-doers
To cheat our lenity with sorrows feigned,
And with impunity to lapse again.
Such penitence is but a lifeless form—
A sterile labour—like a babe dead-born.

    CRIS. It is forgiveness that I crave, my liege,
Not means to sin anew.   Vouchsafe me that,
And in exchange for pardon take my life.

    CON. Would thou wert still a child, for tender age
Has for transgressions, in its helplessness,
Excuse and pardon; while the nerve of man
Makes every foible seem a grave offence.
Yet thou shalt be forgiven.   Thus I tear (*tears warrant*)
This record of my anger, and blot out
Thy past offences by an act of grace.   (*Offers hand.*)

    CRIS. In thanks, dear lord, I kiss your royal hand.
O, let me press you to my heart once more.

    CON. Not yet, not yet.   My mind still smarts and
           burns,
And feels the wales yet of thy scourging tongue.
Time only can assuage and balsam it.

    CRIS. I will with patience, then, your pleasure wait,
And second healing time with fervent prayers.
Meantime, I have a modest suit to urge.
Whilst I, my liege, have languished in your frown,
Your hand has fallen heavy on my friends—
On Mannius, young Licinius, and the rest—
Who, unoffending all, have been confined.
I pray you, sire, your present grace extend

To their enlargement.

Con.   In good time I may.
I'll think of it, I'll think of it.

Cris.   Nay, now—
I do entreat. With me, do what you will;
But, I beseech you, liberate my friends.
I will unmurmuring wait your tardiest will
Ere I will sue you for my lost command.

 Con. (*aside*). Thence come my black and beastly
   fears again.

Cris. Whatever hopes I cherish from your grace
Shall be fulfilled unurged; but free my friends.

Con. Well, well, content thee; I will set them free—
Such, leastwise, as may safely be enlarged;
And for thyself—thy good resolves approved,
No new offences hindering—ere long
My favour may restore thee everything.
My future smiles shall brighten former frowns,
And make thee friends of foes, as summer's sun
Transformeth ugly grubs to butterflies.
Take thou my hand, and come along with me. [*Exeunt.*

ACT IV.

SCENE 1.—Rome. The Palace Gardens. Moonlight.

*Festival, celebrating the twentieth year of the Emperor's
reign. A Minuet, after which the Company gradually
and slowly disperse.*

SEMPRONIUS *and* FAUSTA.

SEMP. The Cæsar gains apace his old esteem,
And will ere long, I fear, if naught be done,
Supplant Constantius in his honours new.
The slightest whisper 'gainst the Cæsar now
Is on the instant checked by Constantine.
Yet jealousy is but asleep in him,
And sleeps so lightly that the faintest praise
Of Crispus starts it; or 'tis sleep assumed,
Where every sense is vigilant, though still,
The ear being sentry to the half-closed eye.

FAUSTA. Now that Constantius is installed in Gaul,
I have no fears for him. This watchfulness
Shows still distrust; and while distrust endures,
The Cæsar's honours will but barren be.
There is no danger.

SEMP.   Something should be done
To keep the Emperor's fear of him alive,
Or, like a lamp neglected, it will die
From want of feeding. If we could revive
The thought that he conspires in secret still,
When Crispus next in anywise offends
(Which in his pride he any moment may),
Belief would, like a millstone to his neck,
Beyond redeeming sink him. I'll away
And see what can be done. Though of myself
I dare do nothing openly, I may

Some whispers set afloat, which, when they reach
The Emperor's ears, not knowing whence they come,
Will set his fears a working.   Fare you well.
  FAUSTA. Against the Cæsar we have rowed too far
In company upon the stream of crime.
He sees I pull no longer, fain to turn,
And takes the scull, determined to go on.
'Tis plain he more than half suspects my aim,
And either must be flattered or subdued,
Or he'll become more dangerous than my lord.
Helena, too—I saw her, worn and wan,
Wasted by misery, and from my brain
I cannot blot the image of her woe—
She has some means encompassed to be here,
And if she meets the Cæsar I'm undone ;
For, though her tongue I bound with solemn vow,
My treachery absolves her from its bond.
Such cheated promises are truths ensnared
In nets that are too rotten to confine.
On every side I am beset with peril.
My past deceit becomes my present scourge ;
My sin corrects itself.   My lawless love
Is pitiful as fierce.   I suffer more,
In sympathy, than he that I assailed,
As if I smote his armour with my hand.
O, what a stake I hazard for this man !
How doubtful, too, the issue yet remains !
While yet unsafe, no bootless blood must flow ;
But, were I once of his affection sure,
I from his meshes would release him still.
What would not disentangle I would rend,
And set a running blood of all my kin
To float him yet in triumph to the throne.
This very night I will determine all.
I have already—in a voice assumed,

Closely enveiled—had happy converse with him,
And was not recognised.   Again I'll try,
And, if disguised I win him, I'll unveil,
To know the most unhappy, or the best. (*Puts on veil.*)

Enter CRISPUS, *musing.*

Now for the trial.   'Tis a heavy stake,
But, to my famished love, as great the prize.
I'll throw the hazard, though I lose the cast.

FAUSTA. My lord.

CRIS.   Sweet mystery!   That voice again?
And still, like muffled music, thickly veiled?

FAUSTA. Not more enwrapt in lace than thou in
          thought.

Why dost thou move and muse so mournfully,
When all men else are revelling in Rome?

CRIS. My heart is sad.

FAUSTA.   Let me essay to cheer.

CRIS. 'Tis heavy-laden.

FAUSTA.   Let me share its load.

CRIS. 'Tis sorely wounded.

FAUSTA.   Let me try to heal.

CRIS. 'Tis dead within me.

FAUSTA.   Let me life renew.

CRIS. Thou canst not that, and shouldst not if thou
          couldst.

Yet would I not seem thankless, and I will,
For these thy good intentions, write thee here,
Upon love's sepulchre, among the few
That I have known as friends—thyself unknown.

FAUSTA. O, write me first; for thou hadst never friend
That loved thee better, or would hazard more
To serve thee, or in serving found more joy.

CRIS. There is a flute-like tremor in thy voice
That makes its note more melting than when firm.
I will believe thee what thou sayst thou art.

I feel thou art a friend, and guess thee fair,
Despite the veil that hides thee.   Thou dost know
My numerous griefs, and pitiest me.

FAUSTA.   I do ;
And pity is akin, 'tis said, to love.

CRIS. Keep, then, thy pity.   Love hath been my foe,
And I distrust his kindred as himself.

FAUSTA. True love, my lord, is enemy to none ;
And tearful pity is beloved of all.
'Tis some pretender that hath been thy foe.
For well I know thou art beloved.

CRIS.   By whom ?

FAUSTA. Not by Helena.

CRIS.   Sully not those lips,
Whose music, spite concealment, proves them pure,
By that once dear but now dishonoured name.
I have loved, lady—not, alas, been loved.

FAUSTA. Ah, yes ; there 's one who long hath loved
            in vain ;
Whose warm impassioned nature yearns for thine
With fervour that her cold heart could not feel ;
Whose arms, forbidden to entwine thee, still
In fancy hourly hug thee to her breast ;
Whose lips, denied the wished-for bliss of thine,
Delight, in speaking it, to kiss thy name ;
Whose longing eyes, when thou art present, seem
To have no purpose but on thee to gaze ;
Who, in thy absence, waking lives on thought,
And sleeping dreams the livelong night of thee.

CRIS. 'Twas thus Helena once did flatter me.
Where is she now, and where her sugared vows ?
Her oaths, like sweetmeats, melted on her tongue.
As false may she of whom thou tell'st me be.

FAUSTA. Nay, she her vows has to another made,
And longs to break them in her love for thee.

CRIS. Then fie upon thy lips to plead for her.
Untrue to him, she would be false to me.
Helena's self is no more false than she.

FAUSTA. An oath extorted under heavy pains
Must not be deemed a pledge of faithful love.
The cursed promise, which her heart disowned,
Was wrung on peril of a life beloved,
And like a tether ties her to a stake.

CRIS. Could I believe this, I could pity her.

FAUSTA. Thy pity breaks her fetter, and she comes—
No faithless perjured lover, red with shame,
But as a fugitive from loathsome bonds—
To offer her still virgin heart to thee.

CRIS. The pleader and the client are the same.
I must dispel this murky lace and see,
As through a cloud, the lustre it conceals.

[*Attempts to remove veil.*

FAUSTA (*preventing him, and twining her arms round
his neck*). O, spare me yet a while! I have a fear,
My face and name revealed to thee, thou mayst
Recall thy pity—heir, I trust, to love.

CRIS. Why shouldst thou fear?   These white and
            tender arms
Are but the envoys of a face more fair.
Now through thy veil two pretty orbs I see,
Which, catching lustre from the pale cold moon,
In warm bright flashes cast it back on me.
Thy breath is sweet—

FAUSTA.   Not sweeter than thine own.

CRIS. Too sweet for aught but beauty to exhale.
What scent conjectures sight shall surely prove.
Though walls conceal their colours from our eyes,
We know by odours when sweet flowers are near ;
Let me break through this stubborn fence, and view
The petals that can give such fragrance forth.

FAUSTA. Thou takest no more sweetness than thou
      givest.
If with my breath thou couldst inhale my life,
In such a way were I content to die.
    CRIS. Nay, I must see. (*Unveils her.*) Great Father!
      Do I sleep?
In mercy rouse me from this frightful dream!
My father's wife!—my mother! Let me go.
    FAUSTA (*clinging*). O, cast me not away. My heart
      has grown,
In this embrace of rapture, to your side.
    CRIS. (*struggling*). Unloose me, wanton.
    FAUSTA. Nay, let me kiss and hug you to relent.
    CRIS. Away, vile woman, ere I fling you from me.
    FAUSTA. Gods! have I cast my modesty aside,
And loved and wooed you, only to be scorned?
You will not love me?
    CRIS.   Love you, wretch? I loathe
Myself and you, for that already done.
    FAUSTA. Nay, then, revenge! (*Runs up stage.*) Help,
      help, help, help, help, help!
    Enter SEMPRONIUS *at the back of the stage.*
Thank heaven, Sempronius, for this timely aid.
Defend me from this monster. Come—away.
               [*Exeunt* FAUSTA *and* SEMPRONIUS.
    CRIS. Abandoned woman, stay—what would you do?
                    [*Exit after them.*

SCENE 2.—Room in the Palace.
Noise without, as of people approaching. FAUSTA *heard*
calling "Help."
Enter CONSTANTINE *and Suite at side; and enter from back,*
in haste, FAUSTA *and* SEMPRONIUS, *with* CRISPUS, PISAN-
NIUS, LUCULLUS, *and others following.*
    CON. What is the meaning of this uproar? Speak.

FAUSTA. O, may the mercy of the gods be praised,
That once again, my husband, at your side
I find myself in safety, chaste and pure.
    CON. What is the meaning—
    CRIS.   Father, give me ear—
    FAUSTA. O, viper! has thy callous soul no shame
To choke the profanation of that name?
    CRIS. Had I, fair devil, half your cause of shame—
    CON. No more of this, but let me know the worst,
Which, should it hit and overtop my fears,
Is bad indeed.
    CRIS.   While walking in the grounds—
    FAUSTA. My liege, as I was walking in the grounds—
    CRIS. I claim to speak, my liege.
    CON.   I'll hear the charge,
And then thou mayst defend—
    CRIS.   How!
    CON.   Silence, sir!
Proceed thou, Fausta.   Be thou brief, but clear,
And tell me that which I'm afraid to know.
    FAUSTA. Fatigued and spent with heat and exercise,
To seek some moments' tranquil solitude,
I wandered from the palace to the grounds,
And scarce had gained seclusion in the shade
Of the luxuriant foliage, when your son
Did thrust himself into my company.
Unwilling to be deemed uncourteous,
I did endure his presence, and concealed
The anger I at his intrusion felt.
But soon his villainous intent I learned,
For round my neck his beastly arm he flung,
And, pressing 'gainst my cheek his filthy lips,
He from my bosom plucked away my robe,
Thrusting his wanton fingers where, save yours
And our dear babes', no hand had been before,

And whispering lecherous love.   I fought and screamed,
When, luckily, Sempronius, sauntering near,
And hearing my distress, rushed up to aid,
On seeing whom your son did loose his hold,
And, feigning indignation, turned on me
As if the shame was mine.

CRIS.   Vile harlot, 'tis.

CON. Hold, misbegotten wretch, thy lawless tongue,
And speak not thus of outraged chastity.

CRIS. Of chastity ?   I charge the gods with shame—
With partial judgment flagrant as your own—
If such a strumpet can remain undamned.

FAUSTA. You hear, my lord, how he would turn on me
The guilty onus of his filthy lust.

CRIS. Impudent wanton !

CON.   Miscreant, hold thy tongue.
Thy breath infects the air.   How paltry poor
Is human judgment for a sin like thine!
Had but my honest indignation power
To visit duly this unnatural crime,
'Twould snatch the lightning from the gripe of Jove,
And strike thee, scorpion, to the lowest hell.
But man is weak, and justice, unappeased,
Must be contented with thy life alone.

CRIS. Weigh not your wrath by what you may impose,
But by what I am able to endure.
'Tis not in scope of your unrighteous spleen
To cause a pang that I can not contemn.

CON. Thou art condemned, defiant monster—

CRIS.   Hold!
I, in the name of hooded Justice (whose
Most sacred wand you were ordained to wield,
But which your warped and biased mind degrades),
Before you speak the sentence, will be heard.
I do not, haughty tyrant, seek to turn

Your lance, already lifted, from it aim,
For I am weary of myself and you;
But to my own integrity and fame
'Tis due I speak, though well I know in vain.
Can your mock justice counterfeit the true
To the extent of hearing my defence,
Or does your proud authority disdain
To give a charged offender leave to speak,
And sentence me unheard ?

  Con.   So I revere
The sacred name of justice, that not e'en
Thy insolence shall weigh with thy offence.
I'll hear thee.

  Cris.   Wondrous charity !

  Con.   Proceed.
Seek not to brave and swagger out thy crime,
But meekly own, or modestly disprove,
The sin charged on thee ; and while thou dost speak,
I will in mercy let mine eyelids fall,
That thy defence and pleading be not marred
By thy most brazen look ; for honest eyes
Do ache to gaze on thee.

  Cris.   Then give me ear,
And as for justice—from the fount on high,
Not from the crook'd and errant spout below—
I look to God, the truth I'll plainly tell.
Some of the revellers, weary of the court,
Sought change and better breathing in the park.
I, sad at heart and soul, did follow them,
But in their boisterous pleasures had no share.
Some talked and laughed, some sang, some danced a while;
Then, what at first was novel waxing dull,
And that which had been irksome seeming new,
They sauntered back into the court ; and I,
Left as I thought alone, wooed solitude.

But soon upon me stole a lady veiled,
Who had before encountered me as then.
I will not tell you with what artful wiles
She took attention prisoner; but I soon,
In the belief that I had found a friend,
Grew interested, pleased, at last enthralled.
Then, grazing first my scars from broken vows,
Which age was healing, she, as if for balm,
Informed me of some richer love, which long
In secret had been nursed for me by one
Who was herself a slave to vows compelled.
And though her lips said " she," while heart meant " I "
(Too modest, simply thought I, to be plain,
But more exposing what she ill concealed),
I, undeceived and curious, tried her veil;
But she, resisting, did implore delay.
Then softly round my neck crept two fair arms,
Into my tingling ears sweet whispered words,
And I, my senses dazed with dainty breath,
At length unveiled her with some gentle force.
When lo, no heart-bruised blushing maid I saw,
Whose pent and timid love pept shyly through
The parted fingers of her bashfulness,
But, with a boldness out of lewdness born,
This hard-faced shameless wanton met my view.

FAUSTA. My lord, you cannot love me if you listen
To this most infamous—

CON.　　　　　Say not a word.
I will with patience hear him to the end,
And show him how, when Justice throbs to strike,
Her heaven-born sister Mercy can forbear,　·
Holding the arm, in righteous anger raised,
Till guilt, self-doomed, invites the stroke of law.

CRIS. I, struck with horror, bade her from my sight;
But still she clung, and wooed, and sought to win;

Then, finding my repugnant loathing firm,
She, with a fiendish cunning, broke away,
And made this heinous charge.

FAUSTA. O, villainy!

CON. Content thee, Fausta. Hast thou said thy say?

CRIS. I have; and now let fall the forejudged stroke,
For, having purged mine honesty with truth,
I would not, to prolong a life I loathe,
Could that appease you, bend my guiltless knee.
But ill must fare the culprit when the judge
Desires the guilt that he pretends to try.

CON. Were thy black crime milk white to what it is,
This hardihood would pluck the heart from grace.
Wouldst on my credence foist so weak a fraud,
That thou couldst hold discourse with her so long,
And yet not know her (though her face were veiled)
By some such trick of gait or turn of form
As marks us all—or, better, by the voice,
Which is a trusty witness to the blind?

CRIS. The veil, which almost to her feet did fall,
As well concealed her figure as her face.

SEMP. (whispering). The veil is safe.

FAUSTA. I have not such a veil.

CRIS. Not now.

CON. No matter for the veil. The voice?

CRIS. Her voice she most consummately disguised.
This she can do.

CON. Why, Fausta, this is true.
Thou hast surprised myself.

FAUSTA. In jest, my lord.
He knows this. 'Tis his craft to speak of it.

CON. What dost thou know of this affair, Sempronius?

SEMP. I know but this, my liege: that when I came
In sight of the dear Empress and your son,
She ran to me, and cried, in seeming fear,

" O, save me from this monster!"

CRIS.   This is true ;

But no less true 'tis that her fright was feigned.

CON. What dost thou think, Sempronius ?

SEMP.   Ask me not ;

For where my love and reverence are weighed

So evenly that half is in each scale,

I dare not trust my judgment to devine

In which to drop the feather of belief.

Pray do not judge from what has gone before.

CON. How else are we to judge, where two oppose

With counter charges, but by character?

Much good of her I know, much ill of him ;

Of her no ill, of him but little good.

And I bethink me now of freedoms past,

Unheeded then, that pointed to this sin.

I solemnly adjudge thee unto death ;

But, as the eye that hath beheld the sun

Some trace of his bright figure will retain

Within the fallen lid, my serried heart

Bears yet a vestige of the foolish love

I bore thee once, and thus much grace I give :

That thou mayst make election of the means

Whereby thou art to die.   To Istria

Thou shalt be sent forthwith, and twenty days

(Under Lactantius' good and holy care) :

I do accord thee to make peace with God,

And ask of him that mercy which in me

'Twould be a sinful weakness to bestow.

If, at the term of these same days of grace,

I be not well assured of thy decease,

The common executioner shall deal

The doom which now my justice hath decreed.

[*Exeunt all but* CRISPUS, PISANNIUS, *and* LUCULLUS.

PISAN. My noble lord, I never did enjoy,

And perhaps did never merit, your esteem,
Which, in the height and heyday of your fame,
I never sought by courtesies to win,
A surly pride restraining me; but now,
In this your hour of agony and need,
Without suspicion I may frankly own
The honour I have ever held you in.
If my poor love and services may meet
Your present need, I lay them at your feet,
And pray you not extrem'st exaction spare,
E'en to the taxing of my worthless life.

Lucul. And at your feet, my lord, my heart is laid.
I never made profession of my love,
For you have seemed to hold me in distrust;
But if, of all in this vain world I prize—
As fortune, life, my freedom, and good name—
There 's aught that may contribute to your aid,
I pray you any, or them all, command.

Cris. Good souls, I thank you for this sympathy,
Which I avouch I never have deserved.
Your generous friendship is of heavenly sheen,
For in my noon of fame I saw you not,
But now, when night and anguish on me come,
You start from out the gloom like shining stars.
But I have done with life and liberty,
And must not, in the remnant of my own,
A useless tribute let you make of yours.
I know not whether grief for mine own blindness
(Ne'er having to my favour ta'en your worth)
Or admiration of your godlike souls,
Which tender all things where they nothing owe,
Affects me most; but this I know too well,
That in your present dignity I see,
As in a glass, my own foregone disgrace.
How speaks it for humanity, my friends,

That those I trusted with my open heart
First fail me in the usances of love;
Whilst you, 'gainst whom my niggard breast was closed,
Press on me that which honour must refuse,
Could e'en acceptance work your noble will?

PISAN. Because we knew you better—

CRIS.   Say no more,
For my reproach is, like a wound that's raw,
So tender that you torture as you soothe.
Yet, simple souls, you are but stocks or staves,
For if you had the busy wits of men,
You could not think thus in this world to thrive.
As stocks and staves I take you to my love—
My bankrupt love—more dearly than as men.
What more is scorned than crutches by the hale?
What more than crutches welcome to the lame?
Such are your friendships to my crippled hopes,
And on your friendships limp I to my end.

[*Exeunt omnes.*

Re-enter SEMPRONIUS *and* FAUSTA.

FAUSTA. He must be saved.

SEMP.   He cannot be.

FAUSTA.   He shall,
Or to my conscience rest can never come.

SEMP. Lay not to conscience what is due to lust.
O, Fausta, Fausta, you dissembled well;
But, though you could bedust your husband's eyes,
You cannot hoodwink me. You love the Cæsar,
And through the mask of modesty you wore
I saw you as his candour painted you.

FAUSTA. He shall be saved.

SEMP.   He shall not, if you live.
You have cajoled me long enough. Beware!
I will no longer be your slave, to gain
The wretched dole of twice divided love.

Your husband's rivalry has been my bane ;
And ere I'll gulp submissively the gall
Of supersession by his stripling son,
I will denounce your perfidy.

    FAUSTA.   Away !
Go—let your fierce malevolence have rein.
I do love Crispus—let the whole world know ;
And rather than outlive him, I will end
A life that runs in harness with his own.

      [*Attempts to stab herself, but* SEMPRONIUS *prevents her.*
    SEMP. Hold, wretched woman ! Are your senses crazed ?
    FAUSTA. They are, alas ! Alas, they are, they are !
    SEMP. Slay nature first ; for raiment, food, and breath,
Are less essential to my life than thou.

    FAUSTA. O, gods ! he must be saved.
    SEMP.   Pledge me but this,
And all the help I can accord I will. (*Whispers.*)

    FAUSTA. Take thou the promise from my lips with thine.
    SEMP. (*kissing her*). O, that the treasures of these lips
          were mine !
Mine only—undivided and entire !

    FAUSTA. O, think we now of Crispus, not of me.
    SEMP. There 's but one way to save him.
    FAUSTA.   What is that ?
    SEMP. I hardly dare to mention it.
    FAUSTA.   What fear ?
The means—the means ?

    SEMP. (*whispering*). The death of Constantine.
    FAUSTA. Why palter thus ? He is already doomed.
If Crispus die, I will not long survive,
And Constantine shall lead the way for me.

    SEMP. Then poison him at once.
    FAUSTA.   Not yet, for then
The Cæsar would at once ascend the throne.

    SEMP. Would you not have it so ?

FAUSTA.   Ay, if assured
That he would seek not to avenge his father.

   SEMP. And what assurance would you have ?

   FAUSTA.   His word.

   SEMP. It is a pledge which one may trust when
        pawned ;
But you esteem him far below his worth
If you believe he'll barter terms with you.

   FAUSTA. The bravery that spits at Death in fray,
When he comes plunging upon lance or sword,
Oft sinks when creeps he shadelike on the dial ;
And honour that in hope shows bright as gold
Will rust, like meaner metals, in despair.
We'll test his boldness and his honour both.
If he will purchase safety on our terms,
You in his favour shall rebellion raise,
Whilst I, to make success more certain, will
Repair to Rome, and poison Constantine.
If he refuse—what then, Fate only knows.
We must to Pola when we safely can.
I will for absence good excuse devise ;
Do thou the like. We'll talk of this again.   (*Retires.*)
This man is needful, as a bridge, to pass
The deep abyss that yawneth in my way.
Once safely crossed, the bridge must be destroyed. [*Exit.*
     Enter OLD HELENA *stealthily, behind.*

   OLD H. Again together.   There is something wrong,
But what, I cannot hear.   I'll watch them well.
She is more guilty than my darling boy.   [*Exit.*

   SEMP. If I do help her, what shall be my meed ?
Assume (though 'tis preposterous to suppose)
That Crispus, cowed and blenching in despair,
Or—sooth, more likely—yearning for revenge,
Should for his vantage fall in with her schemes :
He takes the sceptre, steps into the chair,

Enfolds himself in purple, and commands.
What am I then to Fausta but a bar,
A balk, a block, to stumble o'er, or clear?
Will she, whom marriage fealty could not bind,
Be more exact in truthfulness to me?
I will not trust her; yet I'll seem to aid
While I do thwart her, and will serve myself.
I'll raise revolt, mayhap; but not for him.
I have a scheme, which I have nursed for years,
To seat myself in safety on the throne,
And secret agents have in every land
Whereo'er extends the mighty arm of Rome;
And every hap that bodes these others ill
Is big with promise of good speed to me.
The Emperor, as by her hand, shall die,
And Crispus shall not live. The younger sons
Being yet too crude to govern, I will seize
The reins and sceptre for the general weal,
And, holding her the cause of all these ills,
I'll break her spirit, bend her pride to prayer,
And will extort the homage I have craved.   [*Exit.*

ACT V.

SCENE 1.—Exterior of Fortress at Pola. Moonlight.

BENEVOLENTIUS *and others on guard.*

BEN. This gaunt old fortress, from without surveyed,
Doth in the moonlight wear a sacred air,
But wrong and cruel murder rule within.
The Cæsar's hours are wearing fast away.
The days of grace draw swiftly to their close,
And when thrice more the searching eye of day
Hath looked within these walls, the truest heart
That ever beat for Rome will be at rest.

Enter CONSTANTINE, HELENA, *and* OLD HELENA, *disguised.*

CON. We have out-journeyed them, and are in time.
We will bestow ourselves where we may hear
What they shall say to Crispus. If I find
My strong suspicions are but partly true,
My son shall sit yet higher in my love.

OLD H. 'Tis not suspicion; it is certainty.
Have we not found the veil which she denied,
And proved it hers by witness of her maids?
Have I not seen them talking, lip to ear?
And Servia, Helena's girl, hath seen
Sweet-faced Sempronius kiss your modest queen.

CON. They have at least deceived me in this journey,
And her deceit to Helen bodes the worst.
We'll try the test. I'm glad we are in time.

HEL. We are in time, and yet, perchance, too late;
In time to intercept this guilty pair,
Too late, mayhap, his innocence to save.
O, waste not precious moments.

CON.   Do not fear.
The days of mercy yet are unexpired.

HEL. But he may break his fetters ere his honr.

Con. Why fear the worst, when thou the best mayst
hope ?

Hel. My hopes are topmost, but, alas, not firm.
On ruffled waters sunbeams cannot rest ;
Like them, my bright hopes tremble on my fears.

Con. Come, then ; we'll in, and torture thee no more.

They attempt to enter the Fortress.

Ben. (*lowering his pike.*) Halt ! You pass not without
authority.

Con. We come from the court, on matter of weighty
import. I must see the commander of the fort.

Ben. Constantine himself should not pass without some
intelligible sign. If you were the Emperor, there is not a
man on guard that would not wish his lance in your throat
ere you had time to tell him so.

Con. Is the Emperor so unpopular with his soldiers ?

Ben. Ay, since he has behaved so ill to his son.

Con. I come in the Cæsar's favour; and here is my
authority. (*Shows paper, and whispers.*)

Ben. Enough. You may pass.

[*Exeunt* Constantine, Helena, *and* Old Helena.

Ben. It is Constantine. I knew him well, but I chose
to seem ignorant, that I might slip a bit of truth into his
ears ; and on my soul, if I thought he meant not well, I
would as willingly have slipped my pike into his ribs.

SCENE 2.—Interior of the Fortress.

Crispus *and* Lactantius *discovered, the former at window.*

Cris. Once more the sun upon the sombre east
Begins to paint the picture of the morn.
His vigorous touch breaks up the sullen gloom
With ruby streaks that gleam like bars of fire.
Ah, Phœbus, Phœbus! shall I ne'er behold
Again the splendour of thy handiwork ?
Thou glorious limner, who, upon the wide

And ever-shifting surface of the sky,
Dost paint such wondrous and such varying forms,
In hues so rich and tints so delicate,
Adieu, adieu! Thou paint'st for me no more;
For ere thy round of labour, now begun,
Thou like a wizard endest in the west,
Turning dun vapours into rocks of gold,
Shall I be ended too.

    LAC.   Why die to-day?
Three days of life thy sentence leaves thee still.
Three days of breathing is not much of life,
But in that period great events may come.
Within that time, man's vigour thrice will wane,
And thrice again be quickened by repose;
Within that time, the never-resting tide
Will six times ebb, and times as many flow;
Within that time, the monarch of the day
Will thrice in triumph journey o'er the world;
Within that time, twice reckoned, did the Lord
All beauteous nature out of chaos mould;
Within that time, the mercy of the Lord
May yet redeem thy innocence from shame.
Therefore delay thy sad intent a while.

   CRIS. I am resolved.   Dissuade me not, good father.
Thy ghostly counsel hath girt up my soul,
And taught me through the gates of death to gaze,
With so much hope and little fear as may,
With seemliness, an errant creature dare.
Why, therefore, should I longer linger here,
To lose, perchance, the strength thou hast bestowed?

   LAC. That undue haste may lose no happy chance
Which in the residue of grace might come.

   CRIS. Thou tell'st me to a happier life I go,
Yet wouldst detain me.   When condemned to die,
My father did a certain term accord

To make my peace with God. 'Twas long enough;
And, if forgiveness for my mortal wrongs,
Compassion for the frailty whence they sprung,
And contrite sorrow for what ills I've done,
Be any signs of peace, that peace is made.
Why tax his favour to the latest hour?

LAC. Well, have thy way, albeit my bosom bleeds.
But (I must needs confess it, to my shame)
I cannot, though my mission is to teach
The rendering of good for evil deeds
(The man being stronger in me than the priest),
Look on thy persecutors with the same
Compassionating mercy that thou canst.

CRIS. Grieve not for me, thou good and holy man.
If towards my father in my mind still stays
A thought reproachful, 'tis because thy worth
Hath from his favour yet so sparely gained
That penury seems virtue's only fee.

LAC. Blame not therein thy father. I have these:
Humility, sufficient, and content,
Three things that piety should value more
Than discord, superfluity, and pride.

CRIS. Long live to think so; and what good soe'er
Thou lackest from the brimful lap of power,
Inherit in the grateful hearts of men.
Hast thou provided me the easy means
Of death that thou didst promise me?

LAC.   I have,
But tremble to deliver it. I feel
More like a heartless murderer than a priest.

CRIS. Nay, let me have it. It is kindly done.

LAC. (giving phial). Within this phial is a poisonous
          fluid,
Not nauseous, but of sure though tardy power.
For yet an hour it will as harmless lie

As so much water in thy mortal frame;
Anon will pleasing languor o'er thee steal;
And presently, as gently as a hand
From out an easy glove, thy soul will glide
Out of its earthly prison-house to rest.
May God forgive my part in the sad deed!

CRIS. It seems a marvel that this wretched phial,
These paltry drops, can wreck a soldier's life,
Which all the chances and the shafts of war
Have failed so oft to do. Why, what is death?
What shall I lose in dying?

LAC.   Many things—
Vexations, troubles, slightings, wrongs, and pains—
Whereof the loss is bliss.

CRIS.   And many joys,
Peculiar and distinct to corporal being.
The eye shall lose the green of nature's gown,
With all its rich embroidery of flowers;
The touch shall lose the grasp of friendly hands,
The cheek the vigorous freshness of the breeze;
The ear shall lose the rustling of the leaves,
The sad sigh-music of the laving tide,
The melody of birds, and such sweet sounds
As human art can out of nature tune;
The sense of taste, oft watering with desire,
Shall lose the savour of the various fruits;
The smell shall lose all nature's self exhales,
Or artifice distils, from herbs and flowers;
And that mysterious monarch called the mind,
Whereto each sense is but a serving man,
Shall lose the charms of intercourse with kind.

LAC. All these the senses lose, but in their stead
Succeed, hereafter, spiritual joys,
From the coarse pleasures of the sense as far
Removed as God himself from sinful man.

Cris. Death, slowly coming, to the mind recalls
A legion faults that life and pride ignore.
When sturdy health is bounding through the veins,
And our affairs in this gay world go well,
We're prone to think too much upon ourselves,
Too little on our neighbour, and we wound
His sensitiveness by a hundred whims.
These follies, which as faults we scarcely own,
We write upon our consciences in milk,
And soon forget that which we do not see;
But when the soul is face to face with death,
As if we held the writing to a fire,
They all come out, distinct and black as ink.

Lac. To be unspotted is to be inhuman.
Let not these venial blots disturb your peace.
These, like the shadows in a picture, throw
Our better natures into stronger light.
They are the sins of weakness, not of will.

Cris. I can bethink me of a thousand things
Which I regret, albeit I cannot mend.

Lac. Be comforted, for heaven is just, and will,
When it shall tax the straightness of our way,
Make due allowance for the weights we bear;
And wealth and power are burthens under which
The strong oft stagger and the feeble fall.

Cris. Give me thy hand, Lactantius, while I drink.
I take myself to rest in God's good grace;
And if, in any heart I leave behind,
A thoughtless or ungenerous act of mine
Hath left a foul and loathsome memory,
May charity come, like the cleansing tide,
And to oblivion bear the blot away.
And as I hope this mercy for myself,
So do I now with free forgiveness wipe
And purge away all vengeance from my thoughts.

(He drinks the poison and kneels down.)
Give me thy blessing, father.
Enter behind, unobserved, Constantine, Helena, *and* Old
Helena, *who conceal themselves.*

Lac.   Gentle prince,
If to anoint thee with my own heart's blood
Would save thy life and cleanse thy slandered name,
I would my current of existence pour
Upon thy head, and, as an empty phial,
Would gladly cast my sad heart to the grave.
But I am nothing.   Look we up to God.
O, thou, Almighty and All-merciful,
Look down with pity on this child of Eve.
Against his frailties, let his virtues weigh;
Against his former pride, his meekness now;
Against his sins of malice, his great wrongs;
And if his merits in the poise should fail,
And that the beam unhappily incline
To his disfavour, let thy mercy fall
Into the faltering balance, and give peace.
Bless thee—bless thee—poor unhappy prince.   (*Weeps.*)

Cris. Weep not, Lactantius.   Wherefore weepest thou?
Why should my troubles, fond but foolish man,
Oppress thee with this weight of sympathy,
And force these drops of feeling from thine eyes?
Yet dry them not, but let me look again
Into thy holy lids.   Thou canst not think
How sweet a vision in thy grief I see.
I look into thine eyes, and there behold
A young mulatta, by a father grim
Begot in outrage on a bright-faced dam.
Thy tears baptise it—Pity is its name,
The child of Generosity and Woe.

Lac. O, wring my heart no more, or from mine eyes
I shall beweep my manhood all away.

Is there no trust or legacy of love—
No duty overlooked, no wish forgotten,
No grace to ask, no sign of peace to give—
Which thou to holy duty wouldst confide ?

    CRIS. There is, good soul.   I thank thee for thy care.
Thou know'st, Lactantius, that I loved Helena.

    LAC. I do, my child, and that she loved thee too.

    CRIS. So thought my soul, and joys to think it still.
I was arrested in her presence once,
Upon my father's order, for the death
Of young Basilius, whom in strife I slew,
Which act was cited murder in the writ.
She gave that warrant to the officer
Before my eyes, and hastily withdrew,
And all did seem as if by her arranged.
I therefore thought, and was, moreover, told
(But now I marvel that I did believe),
That she, in secret loving the slain youth,
Had caused my apprehension in revenge.
The wretched Fausta—the unworthy wife
Of him whose honour falsehood said I stained—
She told me this, and much of ill beside,
About Helena ; but since that sad hour,
So fully has she proven her own shame,
And I so much have thought upon it here,
That in my heart the welcome hope has grown—
May nothing blight it !—that 'twas Fausta who,
By some device of cunning, did contrive
To raise this trouble 'twixt us, as a tool
Using Helena.   Motive now is plain.
What dost thou of the Princess know, good man ?

    LAC. I know she wrestles with some heavy grief—
A weight of suffering rather than of shame.
I fear me much her reason is disturbed ;
For o'er her blue eye, once so rich in lustre,

Hath lately hung an unaccustomed haze,
Through which one may discern her gentle mind
Distorted, like a beauteous object viewed
Through flawed and twisted glass.

CRIS.   So sad?

LAC.   E'en so.
She scarcely seems to live, but suffers life,
And with the gentlest meekness.   Her sweet face,
Whence hope seems banished, looketh like a lamp,
A pretty lamp, extinguished.   Sadness seems
So settled on her features, that it shows
Like mourning garments, fitting well with age.
Sometimes she speaks, though not of what she feels—
Her grief is hoarded—but of what she sees.
Discourse with her is simple, but most kind.
She has a treasure of good thoughts and words,
Which she had stored up in her happier days,
Like pearly dewdrops, gathered from sweet flowers,
And in misfortune's hard and horny gripe
She sponge-like sheds them now.

CRIS.   And I the cause!
Since my arrest I have but seen her once—
'Twas just before that dreadful charge was made—
And she essayed to speak to me; but I
Disdained to hear her, and did turn away,
Forbidding her approach with bitter scorn.

LAC. That was ungentle and unjust.

CRIS.   'Twas cruel—
More like a tiger than a reasoning man.
I chid my father in the rudest terms,
And charged him, who with patience heard my plea,
With guilty bias; yet this gentle girl
I have prejudged unlistened to.   Unjust,
I blamed in him the guilt that was my own.

LAC. Too oft is innocence condemned unheard.

CRIS. Were God just only, then the best alive
Would feel the need of mercy.   How stand I,
Who have been both unjust and merciless?

LAC. Make me the bearer of thy word of peace;
For life of man can make no holier end
Than uttering that mercy which he needs.

CRIS. Ay, let me now make what amends I may.
Tell my lost angel I believe her true;
Tell her, but tell her in thy own good way,
That I departed—selfish to the end—
Beseeching her forgiveness.

HEL. (*without*).   It is thine.

LAC. What's that?

CRIS.   Didst hear it?

LAC.   'Twas a woman's voice.

CRIS. I thought it was Helena's, and it said
" 'Tis thine."

LAC.   It may be fancy, yet 'tis strange.

Enter BENEVOLENTIUS.

BEN. Two persons have arrived at the fortress from
Rome.   They have authority to confer with the Cæsar,
and demand to speak with him alone.

LAC. I will retire.   If heaven my hopes confirm,
These people are the messengers of joy.

[*Exeunt* LACTANTIUS *and* BENEVOLENTIUS.

Enter SEMPRONIUS *and* FAUSTA, *disguised.*

SEMP. Good morrow, royal sir.

CRIS.   Ah, is it thee,
Sempronius?

SEMP.   And with him hope for you;
Deliverance, mayhap, from these grim walls.

CRIS. Sempronius, I build no airy hopes
On these fair promises.   Though to mine eye
Thou ever hast a pleasing presence borne,
And seemed most friendly, yet I have observed,

In retrospective thought within these walls,
Whene'er thou busiest thyself for me
Some mischief follows.
    SEMP.   We intend you well.
    CRIS. I stand upon the threshold of a tomb,
And your intents are futile.   Once within,
Nor frown nor favour can affect me more.
Who is this woman, and what would she here?
    FAUSTA. My name is my reproach.
    CRIS.   Thou say'st enough.
My sufferings know thy voice.   What wouldst with me?
Hast thou not wrought enough of ill on me?
Wast not enough to guess my pangs, that thou
Com'st thus into my agonies to pry?
Wouldst thou my meditations turn from grace,
And scare God's holy angels from my side?
I would my brief breath consecrate to prayer,
And thou com'st, like a damn'd incendiary,
To seize the taper of my soul's last hope
And set ablaze its carnal house anew.
Thou art not, surely, woman, but a fiend;
Or thou couldst never thus thy face intrude
Upon my end, to murder peace with rage,
And send my spirit cursing thee to compt.
    FAUSTA. O, it is not to light thy rage I come,
But with my tears to quench it; not to goad
Thy tongue to cursing, but to soothe and save.
O, Crispus, hear me—list—or I must die.
    CRIS. Thou weepest.   I have seen thee weep before.
Thy words come forth in hefts, as if expelled
By strong emotions that contend within.
I've seen thee moved almost as much before.
I have not found thee that which thou hast seemed;
But I would show some charity, and hope
Would fain these signs interpret to be grief.

If 'tis repentance that hath brought thee here
To ask forgiveness, take it and begone,
For I have sluiced my conscience up with grace,
And shut all earthward currents from my soul.

FAUSTA. Conceal thy mercy, and thou show'st it most;
For then thou spar'st me pangs of self-reproach.
This mildness to my gloomy conscience comes
Like dreaded light to secret infamy,
And starts my guilt in blushes to my brow.

CRIS. It is a natural sequence, for remorse
And anguish are sin's footprints on the soul.
But I forgive thee.   Get thee gone, and look
For confirmation of my pardon there.   (*Points upwards.*)

FAUSTA. I dare not look above.   My wretched soul
Can find no comfort but in saving thee.

CRIS. That is impossible.

FAUSTA.   It may be done,
And shall, if thou wilt wink upon the means.
Thy father grudged thy lungs the breath of life,
And long before that accusation came—
Accursed be the hour—he wished thee dead.

CRIS. So said my fears.

FAUSTA.   He seized upon that charge,
Which made an opening for his shaft of spleen—
Long poised and pointed—to assail thy life,
And thrust it fiercely home.

CRIS.   God pardon him.

FAUSTA. Pardon?   O, shame, to speak of pardon now!
Where is the fire that struck thy father's awe,
And made his big heart tremble for his throne?
Art thou so crushed and humbled as to curl
In mean submission whilst a hope remains?
Thou hast a chance to triumph.   Why forgive?
The hand that struck is raised to strike again.
Who pardon needs should seek it ere he finds.

To cry forgiveness 'neath a lifted arm
Is dastardy that begs what it bestows.
'Tis danger proves the soldier. Be a man;
Bestir thyself to conquer. When thy foe,
Subdued and humbled, feels thy strength to harm,
Forbearance then is mercy.

CRIS.   Say'st thou so,
Who art my greatest enemy?

FAUSTA.   No, no.
The wrong I did was wrong, by dread of shame,
Against my wish, and wrecked my peace of mind.
But rouse yourself, and I will yet atone.
Your fate has not been bruited much abroad,
But in the army wonder daily grows,
And many hint in whispers at foul play,
Needing but invocation to your aid
To rise for your redress.

SEMP.   This is most true.
The younger officers are all your friends,
And in the ranks are not a thousand men
That would not quickly rally to your call.
Pledge but your royal word that o'er the past
You will consent to drop a veil of grace,
And we will straightway hasten back to Rome,
And, spreading secret hints of your approach
Among the troops, prepare the way for you.
I have your father's confidence, and here
Your very gaolers are your trusty friends,
Who will, on my instructions, any hour
Unbar your prison gates and let you forth,
Themselves to follow your victorious lead.
Within three days those gates shall be unbarred.
Then march at once for Rome, and on your way
Stout hearts and arms will to your standards crowd,
Like winds auspicious to expanded sails,

And waft your venture to the port of power.

Cris. This would be great and glorious revenge.
To issue from this lone and gloomy tower,
With nothing but my wrongs and sympathy—
To shake the dear old tyrant on his throne,
And when I had the empire of the world
Within my grasp, and at my mercy him—
To lay all at his feet were great revenge.

Semp. Nay, trust him not. Such virtue would offend
And chafe most mortally his envious pride.
Your reputation's growth has been his plague,
Pitting the fair face of his martial fame
With loathsome pockmarks. You or he must die.
Replaced in power, he neither would forgive
Your conquest nor our treason.

Cris. (aside).   Treason 'tis,
But I will probe the filth to its extreme.
And what if I this offer do refuse,
Choosing to perish rather than rebel ?

Fausta. Prefer to perish rather than rebel ?
To die a dastard, while the tyrant lives ?
O, yes, I see—I see thy drift—I see.
Thou wouldst be chary of the dotard's life.
Fool that thou art! thou canst not save him so.
The cursed bond that chained me to his bed—
My hopeful youth to his morose decline,
Like beauty to a bear—I burst away,
For 'tis the root whence all my crimes have grown ;
And if on earth my hate can find a bane,
Thy father shall not long live after thee.
Who triumphs then ? Why, in Constantius' name,
I wield the sceptre o'er the Roman world.

Semp. (aside). Not while I live.

Cris.   Thy guilt hath made thee mad.
My soul must pass in peace. If I were sure

Thy devilish threat would culminate in deed,
I would refuse to profit by thy crime.

FAUSTA. By all that's good or evil, he is doomed.
Thy death avails not him. Then wherefore die?
Thy brothers! Ah! that link is left thee still.
But I will murder them—then kill myself—
And knaves and thieves shall scramble for the throne!
O, that I had but thought of this in time!
I would have swept thy pathway clean of all,
And saved thy priceless life in spite of thee.
Art thou a madman? Hast a reasoning soul?
Seest not what issues on thy life depend?
Thou diest—then this bloody work begins;
Consent to live—thy father's death mends all.

CRIS. Thou sett'st my flesh a crawling on my bones.
Is this the way to purge thy soul of sin?
Dost hope a garment stained with blood to cleanse
By steeping it in gore? To hide the spots
By sullying all the robe is not to clean.
Thou canst not smother sin by heaping sin.
If thou wouldst make atonement, tell me how
Thou didst contrive to rive me from my love;
Make white the name of that dear girl again;
For I believe the treachery was thine.

FAUSTA. Helena? Gods! and is thy soul so mean?
That heartless minx was minion to thy foe.

CRIS. Away, foul slander! I have heard too much.

FAUSTA. Good youth, I never slandered mortal more
Than I belie myself. I am not cruel,
But pitiful, to scorn of life, for thee.
Whate'er I am, thyself hast made me so.
O, Crispus, Crispus—idol of my soul—
Why bar thy breast against my wandering love,
That knocks so loudly for admission there?
O, bid thy heart unlock its gentle gates

And let my travel-worn affection in.
Thy father dead—more justly dead than thou—
Thou shalt his seat by right of heirship take,   •
And change, for thoughts of death and bondage lone,
A life of ecstacy and pomp with me.
  Cris. What ho! Lactantius! Now the mask is off.
I'll balk you, though. What ho! Lactantius! ho!
  Semp. What wouldst thou do, fool?
  Cris.   Justice, if I can.
  Fausta. My dagger—gods!—'tis lost.
  Cris.   Lactantius! come!
Would that thy husband heard thee!
Enter Constantine, Old Helena, Lactantius, Benevo-
     lentius, *and Soldiers.*
  Con.   I have heard
Enough to cure the blind. Perfidious fiends!
  Semp. The Emperor! Ah, then, the end is come.
I will not fall alone though. There—
(Runs to stab Constantine, *but* Benevolentius *receives him*
     on his pike.)
  Con.   Well done.
Thy spleen is baffled. Thou art rightly served.
Thy malice drives its teeth into thyself.
  Semp. The Fates are with you—vain and pompous fool!
Would it were not so, for the Cæsar's sake!
What damnéd accident has brought you here
I know not, nor care now; but let me, dying,
This legacy of comfort leave to you:
That lovely devil was not all your own;
I had your wife, and, had you stayed in Rome,
I would have had your throne ere many days.
  Fausta. O, kill me! kill me!
  Con.   Take the traitor hence,
And let him spit his venom at the wind.
  Semp. While I have speech—this for the Cæsar's ear:

Helena is not guilty.   She believed
Your life in peril, knew you would not fly,
And Fausta, who had wrought upon her fears,
Induced her, under oath of secresy,
To work a little plot to save your life.
She thought the writ she gave the officer
Was forged, and did decree your banishment;
That you would secretly be kept in Rome
Until the cloud of danger passed away,
And she set forth at once to meet you there.
The rest, my lord, you only know too well.
All was by Fausta and myself contrived.
My guilt to you lies heaviest on my soul.
    FAUSTA. Curse on thy craven tongue.
    CON.   Remove her, too,
And let her be confined till we have time
To think what death her matchless crimes deserve.
        [*Exeunt* SEMPRONIUS *and* FAUSTA, *guarded.*
Poor outraged youth, my mind is too confused
With grief and shame for my credulity,
And anger 'gainst the fiends that worked upon it,
To offer consolation ; and thy pride
Hath goodly cause to spurn it at my hands.
But—God forgive me—let the past be buried,
And let the future of itself inform.
          Enter HELENA.
But here is one who, sorely needing it,
Can yet give comfort.   Let your sorrows blend,
Like meeting streams, and be their union joy.
      (CRISPUS *and* HELENA *embrace.*)
    CRIS. My suffering angel! Bless thee. This is joy.
    HEL. O, Crispus, this is rapturous joy indeed !—
Delirious bliss, that waxeth into pain,
As warmth to burning.   Kiss me, sweet, again.
O, saintly hosts, can this rich joy be real?

Or is it but a flash into my soul
Of heavenly light, to leave me darker still ?

Con. No flash, Helena, but a steady flame,　　　　　•
Which long shall cheer thee.

Hel.　　　　　　　　　Yet my busy fear
Already dims it, like an envious snuff.

Cris. Now I can die in peace.　My truth is cleared,
The lost love of my father found again ;
Thy sullied name is cleansed, my doubts are o'er,
And thy fair fame is whiter than before.

Hel. Then all to come is joy.

Cris.　　　　　　　　　Ay, all is joy.
Let me lie down, Helena, for I feel
As I could sleep.　I am fatigued with bliss.　　[*Sinks.*

Lac. O, hapless prince, thy haste has ruined all.
I had forgotten this.　The poison works.

Con. Who talks of poison ?

Hel.　　　　　　　　　Poison, poison ?　Why,
What mean you ?　O, immortal angels ! what—
What poison ?　Who has taken it ?　O, who ?

Lac. Alas, alas ! the Cæsar is to die.
A little ere you came he swallowed poison,
In consummation of that sad decree.

Con. O, most unhappy chance !

Hel.　　　　　　　　　Thou heartless man—
Hard-hearted priest—shame, shame, O, shame on thee.
Thou shouldst console, and thou dost talk of death.
Has earth no ruffian, hell no friendly fiend,
That from that cruel mouth will tear the tongue
That speaks of poison on this happy morn?
I shall go mad—O, heaven—I shall go mad !
And yet he lives.　Thou tell'st not true; he breathes.
O, Crispus, tell this wretched man he lies.

Cris. (*faintly*).　A kiss—a kiss.　Good night.

Hel.　　　　　　　　　Good night, forsooth ?

Why, 'tis but morning yet.   He jests—he jests,
Thou wicked priest.   Men die not merrily;
And Crispus jests, for when 'tis only morn
He says " Good night."   Sweet love, be serious;
For jests are powerless, such deep grief to cheer,
As lighted torches flung to warm the sea.
He sinks—O, heaven—he sinks; and he will die.
Each inspiration 's longer than the last.
See how he gapes, as if to bite the air
That will not let him breathe it.   I have breath;
Take mine, take mine, expiring love—take mine,
And let us go together to the grave.   [CRISPUS *dies.*
He 's gone, he 's gone, and I am here alone—
Unloved and friendless in this world; and still
My stern heart beats.   Who says that nature 's frail?
Alas, it is too strong.   My frighted soul
Yet flutters, like a scared pet in its cage,
In this too tough, too stubborn heart of mine.
Break, break, hard heart, and let my soul go free.
At last—O, mercy!—Crispus—stay—I come.
                    [*Fall on the body of* CRISPUS, *and dies.*
  LAC. Alas, she 's dead.   Like air compressed and pent,
Her swelling griefs her gentle heart have rent.
  CON. Their bones, with better fortune than their bloom,
Shall lie together, in a gorgeous tomb.
I will bemourn them with a grief untold,
And raise their effigies in purest gold,
Whose memory now becomes a lifelong pain,
And in all time to come will blot my reign.

                    THE END.

ERRATA.

Page 10, *line* 34, *read*—
And—but that absence leaves a vacant place.

Page 22, *line* 6, *read*—
Will break the bond and scatter the bouquet.

Page 47, *line* 1, *read*—
And bleach his liver white as he thinks mine.

Page 54, *line* 5, *read*—
Half smiling, too, as tolerant in scorn.

Page 67, *line* 10, *read*—
Then, knowing this, I should such honour prize.

Page 85, *line* 3, *after* "*Fare you well,*" *read*—
Exit Sempronius.

Page 90, *line* 16, *read*—
Thou hast a guilty look.

Page 93, *line* 31, *read*—
Her guardian angel Mercy can forbear.

There are other errors which will be obvious.

www.ingramcontent.com/pod-product-compliance
Lightning Source LLC
Chambersburg PA
CBHW032017010726
47493CB00007B/2450